DANCE OF
S⚽CCER

Bill Berno

Dance of Soccer

Bill Berno

Copyright © 2021 Bill Berno

Published by 1st World Publishing
P.O. Box 2211, Fairfield, Iowa 52556
tel: 641-209-5000 • fax: 866-440-5234
web: www.1stworldpublishing.com

First Edition
Library of Congress Cataloging-in-Publication Data
Softcover ISBN: 978-1-4218-3695-9
Hardcover ISBN: 978-1-4218-3696-6

To Clara

*Thank you for the years of unimaginable bliss
and indelible memories*

"I'm attracted to soccer's capacity for beauty. When well played, the game is a dance with a ball."

Eduardo Galean

THE DANCE BEGINS

Emily knew she was the best player on the Amigos soccer team. Her friends and her grandfather had told her that many times. She loved soccer more than any other sport on earth, and although she had experienced a lot for a 12-year-old, she still hadn't kicked a game-winning goal...and no one knew why.

Today she would have her next chance....

It is a quiet afternoon on the outskirts of Cincinnati, Ohio. Fleecy white clouds form abstract figures to enhance any imagination. Something exciting stirs the peaceful environment, and the air vibrates with an intense rhythm from the cheering and chanting coming from a school soccer field. Two girls' teams are reaching the climax of a close and intense match.

The score board reads, "Scorpions 1; Amigos 0". On the Amigos team, Emily is closely following the #1 player of the Scorpion team, who has the ball and is getting closer to her goal. Emily sees #1 pass the ball to another team member. She realizes #1 is attempting to set up a clear shot for herself. Another Scorpion player sees that Emily is going to try for a steal. The Scorpion player fakes a trip and falls in front of Emily. As quick as a rabbit, Emily jumps over the Scorpion player and steals the ball that is being passed to #1. #1 tries to steal back the ball from Emily, but Emily spins and does an excellent nutmeg through the legs of #1. Then, Emily starts to move skillfully through the ranks of the Scorpion defense by changing directions and changing her pace from fast to slow—slow to fast. The Amigo fans start to chant for her creative dribbling, "Emily! Emily! Samba! Samba!" Brilliantly, Emily has created an open field. She starts toward her goal with incredible speed. The Scorpion team does not have the speed or agility to stop Emily. Finally, it comes down to a one-on-one—Emily against the Scorpion goalie. Emily stops, and with her foot on top of the ball, positions herself for a perfect shot. Throughout the game, Emily has noticed that the Scorpion goalie is right-handed, so Emily moves the ball far to the right. The goalie will have to do a long reach to the left to stop the ball.

With two seconds to play, Emily fires a powerful shot to the left of the goalie. The goalie dives for the ball. It misses her fingers by inches. It looks like the ball is going into the net. The Amigo fans are cheering loudly. At the last second, the ball takes a slight turn to the right, tips the left goal post and bounces out of bounds. The Amigo fans moan as Emily goes down on her knees and covers her face to hide her tears.

Emily's teammates and Coach Brady run to surround Emily. Tears stream down her face. The coach puts his hand on Emily's shoulder.

"Emily, you were great. You stole the ball and then took it all the way down the field. You left those Scorpion girls in the dust with your sambas!"

"Yeah, Coach 'samba'...big deal. I missed the goal. I always do good and then I miss the goal. Maybe I should stick to dancing and forget about soccer."

"You do the hard part Emily. You'll start making those goals soon; I know you will."

Emily's teammates congratulate her on a great game. One of them says, "That Scorpion team knows we should have won. We're better than they are. It was just a lucky wind for them that carried your ball off-course. You did great, Emily. They're probably shaking in their soccer shoes thinking they might have to play us in the finals for the championship."

"Thanks for all your kind words. I guess I'll just have to practice more."

"There's nobody who practices more or practices harder than you, Emily," says one of the teammates.

"Then what's wrong with me? Why can't I make a goal?"

Emily's teammates recognize a rhetorical question when they hear one, so they let it fly in the breeze.

The coach says, "Well, it was a close game. I think we learned a lot. But the most important thing is that, 'We're still Amigos.'"

The girls cheer, "Hip Hip Hooray!" and Emily joins in with a little sadness in her voice, "Yeah...Hip Hip Hooray."

Emily looks around and sees her dog, Fritz. "Come on Fritz! Let's go for a long walk and shake off this lousy afternoon."

Emily walks alone with Fritz. Trees hang low over a walkway that leads to a park. The heavy branches and drooping vines seem to be carrying the weight of Emily's heartbreak. Emily moves slowly through this private tunnel. The thoughts of failure caused by today's lost soccer game torment her so deeply that she cannot even find a tear to soothe her pain. She carries her soccer ball with her and walks with Fritz over to a bench by a small rippling fountain. The peace of the bubbling water begins to calm her.

"I've never made a game-winning goal, Fritz. I don't know why the coach keeps me on the team. Ok, I'm pretty good at defense but that's not enough for me. I want the thrill of making that goal… *of winning the game.*"

Fritz lays his head on Emily's lap.

"Look at our family. Charlie is only two years older than me, and he's accomplished so much already. He's so smart and sweet. He's the pride of the zoo. Everybody knows his name. The animals love him. The elephants come up and greet him. He's even started a fund to raise money for their care if they get sick or need something. Look at me—what have I done? I can't even kick a stupid ball into a stupid net."

Fritz rubs his head on Emily's leg and licks her hand.

"Oh, Fritz you're so sweet. I'm so confused. I don't know what to do. Everybody in our family has achieved so much. Mom's a doctor. Dad's a championship rowing coach. Charlie already knows he wants to be a zookeeper when he grows up. What will I do when I grow up? Who will I become?

"I know they feel sorry for me. They use kind words, but I know what they're really thinking— 'She's no good. She's a loser.' I can't stand that! I want to be somebody they respect. I want to be a champion!"

Emily pets Fritz. "And you Fritz, you're such a big part of our family, and you're the best dog in the world…the best dog in the whole universe! I can't live with my family if I'm a failure. I love soccer too much. It's not just a game for me. It's who I want to be. If I can't be a great soccer player I want to die. I really do, Fritz. I want to disappear from this earth and from everybody. I can't stand it when people come up to me and say, 'Oh, Emily it's ok. You'll make that goal someday.' Yeah, right! When is that day going to come? I'm so depressed, Fritz. I wish a flying saucer would come down and take me someplace where they never heard of soccer, and I'd just be a failure, and nobody would ever know it. Oh, come on, Fritz, let's get going. It'll be dark pretty soon."

Emily and Fritz exit the soothing tunnel of trees and start walking toward town. They come to a busy street. She hears the talking and laughter of some kids. Emily sees about six boys her age near an old garage. They are setting pop bottles on a fence and trying to knock them off by kicking a soccer ball.

As she gets closer, she hears them yelling back and forth. They are betting candy bars, wagering if the next kicker will knock the pop bottle off. She sees a boy kick the soccer ball and miss the bottle. One boy yells out, "Hey, thanks Grease, made five candy bars off your lousy shot."

"Ok, Diesel, let's see you do it. I'll bet all my candy bars you'll miss it too. I know; kick it with your big mouth and you might knock it off this time." The ball bounces toward Emily, and she picks it up. She throws it toward Diesel. "Here you go!"

"Hey, girl would you like to try and knock off a pop bottle? You could win some candy bars."

"I don't eat candy," answers Emily.

Diesel squints in the shadowy light. "Hey, I know who you are! I saw you playin' soccer today. You missed that last goal and you lost the match. Maybe you'll have better luck here. And hey, you could win some really cool candy."

"I guess you didn't hear what I said? But anyhow, no, thanks, I have to get going."

"Chicken! Chicken!" All the boys start 'clucking' like chickens.

"Cluck Cluck! Chicken! Cluck Cluck! Chicken!"

"I couldn't play anyway; I don't have any candy to bet."

"You can bet money."

"I don't have any money with me either. Let's go Fritz."

Diesel goes up to Emily. "Hey, you're a pretty good soccer player; maybe you just had a bad day. I'll spot you the candy. If you lose you can pay me tomorrow. One dollar for each bar. There's about $15 worth here. I'm sure you can scrape that up. You look pretty rich."

"Maybe another day."

"I've got an idea. You don't have any candy; you don't have any money...but you've gotta pretty nice dog there. I'll bet you 15 candy bars, and you can bet your dog."

"Are you kidding me? No way!"

Fritz starts to growl at Diesel then barks and whines as if he is totally confused by the situation. "Hey! I like dogs! I'll take good care of him. Come on. I'll bet you all this candy you can't knock off three bottles."

"Now it's three? Everybody else was knocking off one bottle."

"Hey, you're on a team; you're kind of a professional soccer player."

"Not by a long shot."

"Oh, my mistake. I thought you were pretty good."

"I would never bet my dog! Forget it."

"Ok, guys let's get outta here. She's afraid. Yeah, today I saw you miss that last goal, and it was a pretty easy shot." Emily turns her back to him. Diesel yells at her back, "You better take your doggy and go home and cry to your mommy. You missed that goal today because you couldn't take the pressure. You choked! No guts no glory! And oh yeah, the big reason you missed it...you're just a girl. Let's go fellas." They start to walk away. Diesel starts a chant, and they all join in: "Chick, Chick! Chicken! Chick! Chick! Chicken!"

Fritz barks. "Quiet, Fritz." Fritz barks louder! Diesel turns around. "I think your dog has more courage than you do."

"Hold on a minute. Just wait here. I've got to talk to Fritz."

"Take your time."

Emily takes Fritz to a quiet spot and kneels next to him. "Sit down, boy. This is very important to me." She pats him on the head, "I'm in a tough crisis here. What I want to do...what I have to do is stand up to those lunk-heads, and if I can do that, I'll prove to myself that I can stand up to *anything*. You see Fritz, at this moment in my life you're the best friend I have in this whole world. I know you believe in me, and I know you love me as much as I love you. You're brave, courageous, and you'd sacrifice your life for any member of our family. I know you would. If I'm going to continue to be your friend and your master, I have to prove to myself that I'm worth it. If I don't have the courage to face this challenge—I'm weak. Nobody in our family is weak. That's why I'm going to prove to myself that I can knock those bottles off that fence. I *know* I can do it!"

Fritz barks and wags his tail. Emily calls to one of the boys, "Ok, Grease, set'em up!"

Grease sets a bottle on the fence. Diesel clears his throat and gets very authoritative. "You got three chances to knock off three bottles. If you miss once, you're finished. You lost."

Emily gets ready. She flattens out the ground where she is going to put down the ball. As she is doing this, Diesel explains, "You don't have to worry. I'll take good care of him. I like dogs a lot."

Fritz growls. Emily sets her ball down.

"Hey, what you doin'?" growls Diesel. "You can't use your own ball. You have to use the ball we've all been using. Here, catch."

Diesel throws the old ball to Emily. Emily examines the soccer ball. "I can't kick this old thing. There's not even enough air in it."

"Oh great, here we go with all the girly excuses." Diesel is getting frustrated. "Ok, the bet 's off."

"Ok, give me a practice shot, and I'll see if I can kick it."

"No practice shots!"

Another boy interjects, "Give her one practice shot, Diesel."

"Ok, just one. But not at a bottle. Kick it at the tree and see if you can hit it."

Emily puts the ball on the ground about the same distance as she would have to shoot to knock off the pop bottle. Emily studies the shot with deep concentration and then she starts to run toward the ball. She takes five steps and then kicks it hard. The ball wobbles toward the tree like a wounded bird and then just scraps the side of the tree. Everyone anxiously stands, waiting for Emily's decision. Emily turns and looks at all the boys one by one then looks down at Fritz, "Let's do it!"

Grease puts a pop bottle on top of the fence. Diesel draws a line in the dirt with the heal of his shoe. "Ball's gotta be placed behind this here line or you're disqualified, finished, and the dog's mine."

Emily looks at Diesel. "You go ahead and put the ball down where it's supposed to be, and then I'm sure not to get disqualified." Diesel puts the ball down and moves it a little behind the line. "Do you think that inch is going to make a difference?" asks Emily.

"We have to play by the rules here."

"Right, *your* rules."

"Ok!" shouts Diesel. "Let's go. First shot."

Emily studies the shot. She gets ready. She takes one step, and Diesel shouts out. "I forgot to tell you something. You can only take three steps in your approach."

"Hey, I took five steps when I kicked the ball to the tree, and you didn't say anything."

"Yeah, I let that go because it was practice."

"Ok, three steps. Anything else?"

"Not that I can think of. Go 'head." Again, Emily studies the shot. She looks down at Fritz. With a little smile, she pats him on the head. "Here we go Fritz." She approaches the ball. She kicks it hard. The ball flies directly toward the bottle with good speed and, at the last second, curves slightly up and away from the bottle but touches the top where the cap would be. Emily watches in intense anticipation as the bottle rocks back and forth a few times and then falls backward off the fence.

Diesel exclaims. "That was such a weak shot I don't know if we can count it! Should we count it, fellas?"

The boys huddle together and take about 15 seconds before they say, "Well, the bottle fell off the fence, so I guess we have to count it, Diesel...weak as it was."

"Ok, let her have it," grunts Diesel. "Number two. Set it up Grease."

Emily goes over and scratches Fritz behind the ears, as Grease sets another pop bottle on the fence. Diesel brings back the soccer ball to Emily and starts to hand it to her. Emily points to the line and smiles at Diesel. "Be my guest."

Diesel puts down the ball near the line. "Ok, shot number two." Again, Emily, with deep concentration, studies her shot. There seems to be a strange silence in the area, even with cars and trucks continuously passing by. Emily prepares to take her shot. She looks at Diesel as if waiting for him to interrupt her. Confident that she can take the shot, she takes two steps, and suddenly Diesel calls out, "Hold it! Hold it!"

"What now?"

"Really sorry," exclaims Diesel. "I don't know if I mentioned this very important rule: the ball has to hit the bottle straight on. The ball can't hit the fence and make the bottle fall off like that. Very important!" Emily doesn't respond. "Got it?" asks Diesel roughly.

"Got it!" Emily says just as roughly. She wastes no more time in her preparation. She stares at the bottle and concentrates on the line the ball will travel. With great intensity, she takes the three steps toward the ball and strikes it hard. The ball travels with speed and accuracy as if it were a new ball and not some old piece of leather and cloth. As it approaches the bottle, it again takes a sudden turn, almost missing the bottle, but shaves it on the side to start it spinning around like a top. Everyone is holding their breath. Emily prays silently, "Oh, dear God. Please! Please!"

The pop bottle seems as if it is trying hard to make a final spin. It does and miraculously tilts off the fence. One of the boys jumps up and claps once, then quickly gets a serious look on his face as he turns away from Diesel hoping he was not seen. Diesel pretends he didn't notice. Then he says, "That was so close, we can hardly count it. Fellas do you think we have to count a flimsy hit like that?" They shrug their shoulders.

Emily interjects, "I don't see any pop bottles on the fence, Diesel. Do you?"

"Ok, put up the last bottle, Grease," orders Diesel.

One boy comes up to Diesel holding the soccer ball which is as flat as a Frisbee. "Look, Diesel!"

"What happened?"

"It hit some broken glass behind the fence. What are we going to do?"

"Well," says Diesel, "We'll have to patch it up and finish the contest tomorrow."

"No tomorrow!" charges Emily. "Now! I use my ball."

"Oh, that's not possible."

"Why?" asks Emily in a frustrated tone.

"Because that's not the contest ball, that's why."

"Ok, then. The contest is over, and I'm going home. Let's go Fritz."

"Just a second let's put it up for a vote."

"I think it's going to be a one-sided vote," says Emily.

"No, it won't. Will it, fellas?" They all shake their heads, "No."

"No, I've got a better idea," says Diesel. "We'll use her soccer ball but just to be fair, we have to move the line back a little to adjust for the new ball. How does that sound, fellas?"

They all agree. "Good idea, Diesel. You always got good ideas."

"How far?" asks Emily in an untrustworthy tone.

"Oh, not too far...just a few feet." Diesel moves back about ten feet and draws a line in the dirt with the heel of his shoe.

"Too far," says Emily.

"Ok, I'll move it closer." Diesel moves the line about two feet closer. "How's that?"

"Let's get this thing over with."

"Ok, remember only three approach steps, and once you've started, that's it, you can't stop and start again. Is that clear?"

"That's it! Diesel. No more rules. No more interruptions. This is it! One more interruption and I win! Put the ball down."

There is intense excitement in the small gathering. The twilight is turning into night.

"I can hardly see the bottle," says Emily.

"Oh, it's there for sure. And...no more lame excuses or you'll be disqualified for holding up the game."

"You call this a game?" says Emily.

"Hey, it's so dark; does anybody have a flashlight that they can shine on the bottle?"

Diesel says, "You're holding up the game. I'm ready to disqualify you."

One young fellow holds up a small flashlight. "I got one, Diesel."

"Ok, ok! You stand near the fence and shine it on the bottle. Now let's get this thing over with. I think my new dog is getting hungry," Fritz growls.

"Don't worry, Fritz. We're going home in a minute," Emily says in a calming tone. "Is everything set, Diesel?"

"Yeah. You look pretty nervous?"

"I'm too angry to be nervous."

"Ok, let'r rip!" Emily studies the situation carefully. Without moving, she calculates the steps and speed she will use to approach the ball. She is ready. She starts. She takes one step, and, as she is about to take the second, two things happen simultaneously—1. Diesel gives a loud 'fake' sneeze. 2. A large truck with his high beams on turns onto the road, and his bright lights shine directly into Emily's eyes. Emily shouts, "I can't see! I can't see!" Bravely, she maintains her concentration, strikes the ball hard and stands perfectly still, listening for she doesn't know what. In seconds, she hears it—a glass bottle shattering against the garage door.

She jumps up with joy and hugs Fritz. "My Fritz! My beautiful, beautiful Fritz."

Several of the boys, unable to control their enthusiasm, run up to Emily, pat her on the back and congratulate her with great gusto: "Great shot! Great shot! Here's you ball! Your victor ball!" They pat Fritz all over. "Good boy, Fritz. Good boy. You can go home now!"

"Ok, ok, break it up! Break it up. You got lucky, Girl. I'll get you your candy tomorrow."

"Don't worry about the candy bars, Diesel. You eat them. Maybe they'll make you a little sweeter. And, oh yeah, you better take some vitamin C."

"Vitamin C? What the heck for?"

"Sounds like you might be catching a cold." Emily starts to skip along the sidewalk. "Let's go home, Fritz. I knew I would be able to knock off those bottles. I could never have let you go out of my life...not to a creep like that. I love you too much."

THE NEXT MORNING
THE SUN IS SHINING

Emily runs out of the house with Fritz barking and chasing close behind. Emily goes into a small stable and walks out leading a beautiful palomino horse. "Come on, Pegasus...ready to run?" Pegasus whinnies, and Fritz barks in reply as Emily climbs onto Pegasus who's bareback. She takes off in a gallop. As Emily, Pegasus, and Fritz move through the countryside, she begins to feel better. She notices how the sea-green grasses swell like a lazy ocean wave along the rolling hills. She spots a young Chinese girl holding the hand of an older Chinese man as they walk along a path in the Ohio woods.

The Chinese girl looks up, sees Emily and waves to her. She pulls on the arm of the man. "Look Father! See girl on beautiful horse. She ride beautiful."

"Yes, Ming, she rides beautifully. It looks like she floats on air."

"Father, she dance too. I see her in town through dance-school window. She beautiful dancer too. She do ballet and also rock and roll. She very talent."

"Rock and Roll well...she *must* be talented," he chuckles to himself.

"Oh look, Father. She come this way."

Emily rides up to Ming and her father. "Hi! How are you? Are you enjoying a walk in the woods?"

"Yes," says Ming, "You ride beautiful on beautiful horse."

"Thank you."

"What horse name?" asks Ming.

"My horse is named Pegasus."

"Oh, Pegasus." Ming's father says. "He was a Greek mythical, winged divine stallion, 'The King of Horses,' I think they called him."

"Yes, sir. You are very smart," says Emily.

"No, I love the Greek stories," replies Ming's father.

Emily dismounts from Pegasus. Emily notices that Ming is as tall as she is. "My grandfather wanted me to name him Neptune who was worshiped by the Romans as a God of horses. But I told him, Bibou, he's a horse—not a fish."

They all laugh. Ming asks, "Who's Bibou?"

"That's what I call my grandfather. He likes that name. Oh, and this is my dog, Fritz. Say 'hi' Fritz." Fritz barks and wags his tail. "Anyway, welcome to our beautiful countryside. My name is Emily. What's yours?"

"My name Ming, and my father, Dr. Yang."

"Pleased to meet you. I haven't seen you at school, Ming."

"Not yet. I come soon."

"We have to get all the papers together. We've only been here a few months," Ming's father explains.

"Where are you from?" Emily asks.

"We from China," Ming says proudly.

"Wow! That's a long way away," says Emily. "I've heard that if you dig a hole straight down from here and keep digging and digging, you'll finally get to China."

"That might be true," says Dr. Yang, "But, flying in an airplane is much faster."

They all laugh. Emily mounts Pegasus. "Sorry I have to be moving along. My dad has a regatta this afternoon. It's for a championship, and I don't want to miss it."

"Oh, is it a sailboat race?" asks Dr. Yang.

"No these are long boats with eight men rowing. They're called an eight-person shell. They're 62 feet long."

Ming gets very excited. "That really sound like fun. Can we go see race, Father?"

"I'd love to Ming, but I have an appointment at the hospital..."

"Oh, I'm sorry. Is everything ok? You look so healthy."

"Oh no, thank goodness it's not that," he chuckles, "I have appointment to see my friend from China, Dr. Liang, who works at the hospital. He's a surgeon."

"Oh, my Mother works at the hospital too. She's also a doctor. She's an anesthesiologist. Well, this works out fine. I'll go to the race and then to dance class and then soccer practice after school. After that, I've got to do my homework because I've got a test tomorrow. I'll look forward to seeing you at school, Ming. Maybe someday we'll go riding?"

"That would be great! Do you think it would be ok if I watch your soccer practice?" asks Ming.

"Sure, that would be fine. A lot of friends and family come to watch our practice. So nice meeting you both. Bye!"

Emily mounts Pegasus, nudges him, and they take off in a gallop. Fritz barks as he catches up to Pegasus. Ming and her father wave to Emily and her animal friends. Emily stops, turns Pegasus around, and waves to Ming and her father. As Emily watches them start to move down the path, she notices that Ming walks with a limp in her left leg.

EMILY AT SOCCER PRACTICE

Emily runs up to the soccer coach, "Coach Brady, are you going to move me to offense? You said if I did good in yesterday's game I would be moved to offense."

"Well, you did very good, Emily," says Coach Brady.

"I know, but I missed the big chance to tie the game. I know I blew it."

"I don't think you blew it, Emily. I think the wind blew it." He chuckles.

"Yeah, right, Coach," harrumphs Emily.

"Right now, we need you on defense, Emily. You're really good at stealing the ball away from the other teams and you're quick, agile and an excellent dribbler."

"Yeah, but I can't make those dog-gone goals!" Fritz barks. "Sorry, Fritz."

The coach looks around. "Harvey! Where the heck is my soccer boy?" Then a young husky boy, carrying more soccer balls than he can hold and some red cones, comes running up to the coach. "Harvey, hurry up and get those cones planted for the cone drill."

"Ok, Coach. Right away."

"Then get the balls ready for the point drill."

"Ok, Coach, I'm on it."

"Good boy, Harvey. Too bad you're not a girl. I'd have you on the first team." All the girls laugh as Harvey gets red in the face. Harvey places 20 cones in rows about 10 feet apart.

"Ok, Amigos. You know the drill. You dribble the soccer ball back and forth as you proceed to the end of the cones and then turn around and come back. I know that's really difficult, but it's good practice to improve your coordination."

Some girls are slow as they try to dribble quickly through the cones. Emily takes her turn, and she is very fast and shows good dexterity. She stops sometimes and fakes as if she's going left and then goes right.

"Those are good feints, Emily," says the coach. "Girls watch how Emily does those feints. You've got to learn those so you can fake out your defenders. Fake left, go right, fake right, go left. You'll get it."

Emily dribbles quickly to the end of the stakes feinting as she goes. At the end, she doesn't turn around but dribbles the soccer ball behind her. She is very agile as she makes her way back to the starting point. When she gets to the end of the drill, all her teammates applaud and shout, "Way to go, Back-door-Betty!" Emily smiles and swings her fist over her head.

Then the coach and Harvey set up the soccer balls so the girls can practice kicking them into the net. Emily kicks the balls hard and sends them into the net time after time. Emily calls to the coach. "Coach, I don't understand it. I do really good in practice. Why can't I make a goal in a game?"

"It's a mystery to me too, Emily. I can't figure it out. Maybe it's nerves. You're perfect in practice, but in the game...I'm sorry... don't know why." The coach blows his whistle. "Ok, team. Good practice! You're lookin' ready to meet your challengers at the tournament."

One of the girls looks worried. "I hope it's not the Terminators. They're really good, and that #13 is really big and tough."

"Well, you know what they say, *the bigger they are, the harder they fall.* Whoever it is; we'll show'em how to play soccer! Right Amigos?"

"Right Coach!"

The coach calls to Harvey. "Harvey, get the balls and gear together, we gotta big game tomorrow. Shine up those balls tonight. Ok?"

"Ok, Coach...but ah... I have to tell you something. My dad got transferred in his job, and we've gotta move to a little town in Northern Ohio, called Holgate. My dad told me I have to start packin' up the house tomorrow 'cause he's drivin' down to Holgate to see if he can find us a place to live."

"Funnily enough, Harvey. I grew up just outside of Holgate on a farm, and I knew a lot of people there. I even knew this family that lived next to the Catholic church by the name of Brunos or Bermos. I could never remember that name. We used to call them the Bermoseltzers. There were two twin boys who were very intelligent, and then an older boy who was very strange and not too good in school. They tried to keep him out of the public eye. He slept in the attic. He was a loner. They say he trained the mice up there to swing on trapezes. He was going to take them on tour, but the neighbor's cat kind of upset those plans. You know, he was the only person in the history of Holgate who failed to graduate from high school because he couldn't say the alphabet in the correct order— like everybody else learns to do. He claimed he knew all the letters, he just couldn't remember them in the normal order, like 'A, B, C etc.' He made up his own rhymes, but his teachers wouldn't accept them—kind of sad.

"Anyhow, their father ran the restaurant and bar. He was also a sign painter, and he knew all the people in town. So, have your dad give me a call tonight, and I'll tell him how to get a hold of this guy. I know he'll be able to help your dad find a home for you guys. Also, your dad might want to stop in Bruno's bar, or whatever it's called now, 'cause they've got the best coleslaw in Northern Ohio."

"Thanks, Coach. I hope you'll be able to find somebody to take my place. I guess you realize that my sister, Claudella will also be going."

"Those are tough shoes to fill, Harvey. But I'm sure we'll find somebody. The soccer gods are always watchin' out for us. Take care and good luck, Harvey, and tell the same to Claudella."

Harvey walks away with a sad look and then turns and smiles to everyone. "See ya, Amigos. I'll miss you. You're a great team!"

They all wave back to Harvey and throw him kisses. "We love you, Harvey!"

The coach waves to Harvey. "Good luck, Harvey!" Then he turns to his team. "Amigos, we're going to have to find a new soccer boy and a new captain for our Amigo team. You know what they say, 'Life is like soccer. You get kicked around a lot but then someday, somehow, that ball ends up in the net.'"

A lady walks up quickly to the coach with an envelope in her hand.

"Oh, hi honey! Everybody, I want you to meet my wife, Jenny!"

"Hi, Jenny!" everybody responds.

Jenny says, "Honey, this letter just came for you. It looks like the one you've been waiting for from the soccer committee. I thought it might be important, so I brought it right over. I'm sure the girls will be excited to know what it says."

"Open it Coach, open it!" The girls shout excitedly.

"Ok, ok...take it easy. I'll open it!" The coach reads it to himself and then gets a big smile on his face. "We've been picked to play in the Ohio Soccer Tournament, and the winner gets a trophy."

All the Amigo girls jump for joy! "Who are we going to play, Coach? Who are we going to play?"

The coach gets a half-a-smile on his face. "Well it looks like... we're going to play...the Terminators!"

"Oh, no..." the girls exclaim sadly. "Not the Terminators! Their #13 is so good and they're all really tough and really big!"

"We can beat'em. I know we can." says the coach. "Our team is looking sharp these days. Fast and agile can win over big and tough. I've seen it many times. Nothing to worry about."

"If you think we can beat them, Coach," says Emily, "We know we can beat them. Right girls!!!"

"Right Coach! We can do it." All the Amigos cheer.

EMILY AT DANCE CLASS

"Thank you so much, Ming."

"You so graceful. What you call that spin you were doing?"

"A pirouette...but I can do better. I know it takes years of practice. I'm just getting started but thank you so much. You want to have some fun, Ming?"

"Sure!"

"Let's go over to the trampoline."

As they approach a large trampoline in the corner of the room, Ming's eyes get bigger and bigger with excitement. "Wow! I never see such big trampoline!"

"That's a 15-footer. Have you ever jumped on a trampoline, Ming?"

"Not this big! Not this big!"

"Watch. I'll show you, and then you can try." Emily jumps up on the trampoline and starts bouncing higher and higher and then with her body in full extension she does a perfect back flip and comes down gracefully landing on both feet.

"That is beautiful, Emily. I could not do that."

"I've been bouncing on this trampoline for over a year. It's not hard. Don't try a flip yet—just bounce on it. It's so much fun." Emily jumps down, and Ming swings herself up onto the trampoline.

"Pretty good mount, Ming!"

Ming smiles and starts bouncing high on the trampoline. Effortlessly, she lays her body out flat and appears like a butterfly suspended in flight. She seems weightless.

"Beautiful Ming, beautiful!" exclaims Emily.

Then Ming makes a perfect landing on the trampoline with both feet and then dismounts.

"Wow, Ming. Have you ever seen someone do a Butterfly Kick in soccer?"

"Oh yes."

"It looked like you were going to do a soccer butterfly kick. It looked like you were flying, Ming. That's what it looked like to me."

"It feel like that too." says Ming.

"You must have been on trampolines before."

"China have many trampoline, but not this big."

"That was really fun. I've got to get to soccer practice. Would you like to come and watch?"

"I love to," smiles Ming.

SOCCER PRACTICE

Emily and Ming are standing with the girls of the Amigo soccer team who are practicing dribbling the soccer ball and kicking it back and forth. Coach Brady comes on the field and gets into the circle of the girls. "Well girls, I've got some good news and some sad news."

All the girls look worried, "Oh, no coach. What's the matter?"

"Well first, the good news." Just then a tall girl with long red hair comes onto the field and joins the rest of the team. "Oh, look," says the coach. "It's Veronica! Girls, I want you to meet Veronica. Veronica, this is the Amigo soccer team."

"Hi, Amigos!" waves Veronica.

"Hi, Veronica!" cheer the Amigos.

"I met Veronica and her father the other day, and Veronica would like to join our team. And her father is going to buy us new soccer jerseys."

"Oh, great!" exclaims the Amigo team.

The coach continues, "I think a few of you girls have met Veronica."

"Yeah, we have," says Brenda Jean. "And guess what? The coach made Veronica the new team captain."

"No, Brenda Jean. I said, we as a team would vote for a new captain. Now is there anyone else who would like to be the captain of the Amigos? Just raise your hand."

None of the girls raise their hand. Then, shyly, Emily raises her hand. As she does, Ming, with a big smile, claps her hands several times. Brenda Jean gives Ming a dirty look.

"Ok, ok" says the Coach. "Is there anyone who would like to say something about the two girls who would like to be captain of the Amigos."

"I'd like to say something," says Brenda Jean.

"Ok, Brenda Jean go ahead," says the Coach.

Brenda Jean clears her throat. "Well, I'd just like to say, Emily is a really good player...on defense, but she's had a lot of...I mean she's had some problems making goals. Like in our last game... it was close, but she missed our big chance to tie the game in the final seconds." Emily looks down at the ground in embarrassment. Brenda Jean continues, "On the other hand, Veronica was on the girls' State Championship Soccer Team last year in San Francisco, and she was the captain of that team, so I feel it would be really inspiring for the Amigos to have someone as good as Veronica for our captain. Let's vote!"

"Wait a minute. Wait a minute," says the coach. "Does anyone have anything to say about Emily?"

All the girls on the Amigo team are silent and don't look in Emily's direction. Then Ming speaks up loudly with a big smile. "I think Emily make good captain. She very smart!"

Brenda Jean puffs up. "Hey, you're not on our team! This is just for the Amigos."

"Take it easy, Brenda Jean," says the coach trying to keep the meeting cordial. He then turns toward Ming, "I'm sorry, but Brenda Jean is correct."

"Sorry," says Ming quietly.

"No problem," says the coach sweetly. "Ok, Veronica and Emily go over by the bench and face away from the field."

Emily and Veronica walk over by the bench and stand quietly. Veronica is facing the field. Emily whispers something to her, and Veronica spins around with a little huff.

"Ok, girls now we're going to vote by a show of hands. Raise your hand if you would like Emily for your captain."

Only two girls raise their hands. Ming looks sad and raises her hand high. Brenda Jean runs over to Ming and pulls her hand down roughly while giving her a dirty silent look. Ming brushes off the arm that Brenda Jean touched.

"Ok, girls now we'll vote for Veronica. If you'd like Veronica for the Captain of your Amigo team, please raise your hand."

All the rest of the girls raise their hands and can't contain their excitement. "Veronica's our new captain! Yeah for Veronica! Hip Hip Hooray!"

Veronica turns back toward the team and raises her fists in triumph.

Emily says quietly, "Congratulations."

Veronica ignores Emily and runs back to the team. Ming goes over to Emily and gives her a big smile and a hug, "I know you be better captain."

"Thanks, Ming. We'll give Veronica our support and see how she does."

"Congratulations, Veronica," says the coach, "I'm sure you'll make a fine captain. Now, we've got a little more business to attend to girls. With Herman also moving away, we need a new soccer boy. Does anyone have any ideas how we can find a soccer boy quickly? We've got some important games coming up."

"I be soccer boy!" Ming exclaims enthusiastically.

Veronica and the other girls laugh. Emily says, "Why are you laughing? Ming is very talented."

Veronica says, "You don't have to be too talented to know the difference between a soccer ball and an egg-roll." The other girls laugh.

Ming says, "I know difference!"

The coach says, "Ok, girls. Be nice." He walks over to Ming. "I heard Emily called you Ming. Is that your name?"

"Yes, sir."

The coach asks, "Have you ever seen soccer?"

"Oh, yes. Soccer very popular in China. Everybody play."

"Did you play, Ming."

"Yes, Sir."

Veronica cuts in, "With that limpy leg?"

Emily responds, "Hey, Veronica!"

Veronica says, "What?"

"That wasn't very nice for the new captain of our team."

"Are you her mother?" asks Veronica.

"No! I'm her friend."

The coach interjects, "Ok, girls. We can't have this kind of talk." He looks at Ming, "Ming, if you'd like the job of soccer boy, we'd like to give you a try. Would you like that?"

"I love that!" smiles Ming.

"Good. Ok, Amigos let's come together for a team cheer." Coach Brady puts out his hand and all the girls put their hand on top of his.

Emily looks at Ming. "Come on over, Ming. Put your hand on mine."

"That's right, Ming," says the Coach, "Even the soccer boy, I mean soccer girl, is a member of the team."

Veronica raises her eyebrows.

The coach says, "Ok, girls on three. One, two, three."

Emily whispers something to Ming.

All cheer, "AMIGOS!"

Coach calls to Ming, "Ming I want you to do something as your first night as soccer girl."

Ming responds, "Yes, sir."

The coach asks, "Ming, have you ever cleaned a soccer ball?"

"Oh, yes sir, many time."

"Tell me how you do it."

"The way I do is first wipe ball with damp cloth. That take off scuff marks. Then dry ball and see if more marks. After that, get warm water—mix mild soap, no use bleach—dip sponge in soapy water and scrub tough scuffs away. Then dry ball with dry cloth. It look like new. Guarantee!"

Happy with Ming's response, the coach says, "Excellent, Ming. Take this dirty soccer ball home tonight and see what you can do with it. I think you're going to make a great soccer girl!" He lobs the ball over to Ming.

Ming stops the ball with her thigh and then bounces it high up a few times with her knee and then finally spins around and catches it behind her back. "Thank you, Coach!"

"Pretty good, Ming." The coach gives her thumbs up and turns to his team. "Ok, Amigos. That's it for today. You can practice your dribbling and shooting into the net for a short while and then I'll see you tomorrow. And hey, don't worry about those Terminators. We'll terminate them!"

After the coach has left the area, Veronica calls to Ming. "Hey, get me a Coke, Minn."

"It's Ming, Veronica, not Minn. She's from China not Minnesota," says Emily.

"Oh, little miss Geography whiz..."

The other girls chime in, "We all want Cokes."

Emily starts to instruct them. "Too much sugar isn't good for you before a game or practice either. It's going to give you false energy, and then after halftime in a game, you're going to crash."

"Oh wow! Now she's also a nutritionist."

Ming interjects, "Right, her mother doctor!"

Veronica sarcastically says, "Oh, really. My mother is a clothing designer for young women, and she's got a nationally syndicated business with shops in San Francisco, LA and New York to mention a few."

Some of the other girls exclaim, "Wow that's so cool! What's the name of the..."?

Veronica interrupts, "Oh, didn't I tell you? It's called, *Veronica's Dove.*"

The other girls yell, "Oh, that's so cool! Veronica's Dove!"

"Haven't I shown you my brochure yet? Silly me. I've been so busy." Veronica pulls a brochure from her small purse. She holds up the brochure to the girls. It shows Veronica posing in a beautiful dress with a white dove on her shoulder.

The other girls ask, "What a beautiful dress, and look at that white dove on your shoulder! Weren't you afraid?"

Veronica smiles, "Oh, no. They are specially trained not to bite."

Ming turns to Emily and in a soft voice says, "I hope it trained not to leave souvenir on shoulder."

Emily chuckles with Ming.

Veronica sighs, "Hey! I really need a coke that's *if no one minds,*" giving a sarcastic glance in Emily's direction.

The other girls yell, "Yes, Cokes! Cokes! Cokes!"

Ming, says, "I get Cokes, Emily. No worry."

"I'll help you, Ming," says Emily staring darts at Veronica. "Oh, I left my money in Daddy's convertible. Does anyone have a dollar I can borrow?"

"I'll buy you a coke, Veronica," says Brenda Jean. "That's the least we can do for our new captain!"

"Oh, that's so kind of you. What's your name?"

"Brenda Jean, and welcome to our team." Brenda Jean giggles.

"Did you hear that? I made a rhyme! Come on Amigos, let's cheer for Veronica!"

They all cheer together as Emily and Ming cheer quietly under their breath, "Veronica! Veronica! Our new team captain."

Emily and Ming get the change from all the girls. They go to the Coke machine and get as many Cokes as they can carry. They bring them back to the other girls. The girls go over to the picnic tables and start drinking their cokes as Emily and Ming practice their dribbling and shooting the soccer balls into the net. From across the way, two young boys about 12 years old are watching the girls practice. They take off their jackets and wrap them around their waist like skirts and then talk and laugh, making fun of the girls. They have a soccer ball and kick it all over the bleachers in mockery. After about 10 minutes, Emily calls to her team members, "Hey, Amigos, aren't you going to come over here and practice your dribbling and kicking like Coach wanted us to?"

"I guess..." they moan and slink over to the soccer field. They all start practicing kicking into the net as they continue drinking their cokes and missing most of the shots.

Emily says, "Why don't we finish practice by running a few laps around the soccer field?"

The Amigos start enumerating their excuses. "I think I have to go. I've got a lot of studying to do," says Brenda Jean. "Anyhow I'm getting a stomachache. I had a big lunch."

Other Amigos start walking off the field, "I'm getting a headache," says Laura.

"I really, really don't think I should run right now," says Barbara. "Maybe tomorrow," she adds as she walks off the field fast.

A car horn sounds from the street. "Oh, that's my daddy," says Veronica. "I've got to go, girls. I'll see you all tomorrow. Bye!"

The remaining Amigos wave goodbye to Veronica.

ON THE WAY TO MING'S HOME

The sun is starting to set as the rest of the Amigo team says goodbye to each other and exit the soccer field. Ming turns to Emily: "Emily would you like to come and see where I live with father?"

Emily answers, "I really should get going myself."

"Father will give you ride home. He said would be nice if I brought you over to see house."

"Ok, I guess it won't take too long, and then I'll be home soon. Thanks a lot, Ming."

"Mei Wenti," says Ming.

"What did you say?" asks Emily.

"Mei Wenti...it means 'no problem' in Chinese."

"Mei Wenti," echoes Emily. "I like that. 'Mei Wenti.' I want to learn some more Chinese words.

"Ok, great! I teach you more words on way home. Go this way. I know shortcut through woods."

Ming and Emily start through the woods. It is getting darker by the minute. Suddenly, the two boys that were mimicking the Amigo girls' soccer team jump out from behind a tree. "Hi, Ladies. Out for a little stroll tonight?" says one of the boys.

"We're on our way home," says Emily.

"Maybe we should walk ya. Sometimes at night there's boogie men in these woods."

Emily says, "I think we're fine. Thank you very much."

"We'kin protect ya. We ain't afraid. Right, Grease?"

"Right, Diesel?"

"We really have to be going. But, thanks for the offer," says Emily.

"See how nice she talks, Grease? Why don't you learn some nice fancy talkin' like that? Then you'd be popular with all the girls."

"Think so, Diesel?"

"I know so, brother." Says Diesel.

"Oh, you brothers?" asks Ming.

"We're cousin's, but we're like brothers. Right Brother?"

"Right, Brother!" says Grease

Ming points to Diesel. "You Diesel." Then points to Grease. "You, Grease. Right?"

"You're pretty smart," says Diesel.

"Where you from?"

Emily interrupts, "We have to be going."

"See how nice she sounds, Grease? 'We have to be going.' Not, 'We gotta get goin.' Like you talk Grease. Diesel looks at Ming. "Where'd you say you were from?"

Emily is getting a little concerned. "She didn't say. And sorry, but we have to go."

Diesel says, "That's not polite, right Grease? Let's see... looks like she's from someplace like Japan or China. That right?"

"China," says Ming.

"Me and Diesel we like Chinese food. Right Diesel?"

In a strong tone Emily says, "Good for you, brothers! We gotta go!" as she mimics them.

"Hey, hold on a minute!" says Diesel. "We know you, girl," he continues while pointing to Emily. "I almost won a real nice dog from you. I should'a got that dog. Your kickin' wasn't that great."

"Let's go Ming. See you fellas later, and then again, maybe we won't."

Diesel eyes the soccer ball Ming is carrying. "Say, that sure is a real nice, fancy new soccer ball you got there, Little Miss Chop Sticks. Can I take a look at it?"

Ming and Emily speak in unison, "NO!" Emily is starting to leave. "Come on, Ming."

While the conversation is continuing, Grease makes his way behind Emily, and he gets down behind her on his hands and knees. Diesel puts on some airs, "Well you two ain't bein' very neighborly. Is that the way you treat strangers in China...Ming? Isn't that what your friend called you? We just wanna be friends with you's."

Emily tells them, "Well you're no friend of ours. And you know what, Diesel?"

Diesel with a fake smile, "See how nice she is, Grease? She even knows my name already. They're startin' to get neighborly. We just wanna be friends, right Grease?"

Emily says, "You know what?"

Diesel shoots back, "Not yet..."

Emily says, "If you take the 'r' out of 'friend' you get, 'fiend'".

Grease answers, "You know what that is? Is it this?"

Grease is now behind Emily on his hands and knees. Diesel pushes Emily and she falls backward over Grease. Ming shouts, "Very bad! Very bad!"

Diesel laughs, "Oh, yeah. What you gonna do about it? Now let me have that soccer ball!"

Ming holds the ball up toward Diesel. "You want? Here!" Ming places the ball down on the ground and, with a powerful left foot kick, she sends the soccer ball with tremendous speed and hits Diesel in the head. Diesel grabs his head and kneels on the ground. The ball bounces back to Ming.

Diesel holds his head in pain, "Get her Grease! And get that ball!" Grease spreads his arms like he is going to engulf Ming and growls as he goes toward her.

Again, Ming puts the ball on the ground. "Ok, Grease. I bet you good catcher, right? Catch this!" And again, with tremendous power Ming blasts the soccer ball directly into Grease's stomach.

Grease buckles to the ground gasping for air. "Can't breathe, can't breathe."

Ming gets the soccer ball and runs over to Emily. Ming holds out her hand and helps Emily up as Diesel and Grease lie panting on the ground like two old dogs who have lost their way in the muddy banks of the Mississippi.

Ming says, "Let's run, Emily!"

Emily says, "Can you run ok, Ming?"

"Watch me!" They start to run down the dark path. Ming limps as she runs, but she is keeping up with Emily. After running about 25 yards they stop, turn around, and Ming says, "No more Diesel, no more Grease."

Emily answers, "Good!"

Ming says, "Come on Emily, let's run! I know short cut to house from here."

They start down the dark path. Emily notices that Ming is a good runner even with her limp. "You're a good runner, Ming."

"Oh, yeah, I had to learn a new way of running after I got hurt."

Emily slows down. "Ming, I have to slow down my right leg hurts a little bit."

"You ok, Emily?"

"I think so. I guess I hurt it when Diesel pushed me."

"Here, let me help you. Rest on shoulder." Emily wraps her arm around Ming's shoulder, and they continue walking down the path.

"Before we go on Ming, I want to thank you for helping me back there. I would like to say, 'thank you' in Chinese."

"Very easy to say, 'thank you' in Chinese. It sound like this, *Sh-yay* and spell *xie xie*."

Emily practices the pronunciation, "*Sh-yay Sh-yay*."

"Very good, Emily. You have good ear."

"*Xie Xie*, Ming. This is fun. I would like to learn a little every day."

"*Mei Wenti*, Emily."

"That's right, Ming. *Mei Wenti*, 'no problem,'" they both laugh.

"Very good, Emily," Ming, laughs, "I think those guys not coming."

Emily returns, "You're right. You really clobbered them. Where did you learn to kick so powerfully?"

Ming says, "Oh, I play soccer in China and Father taught me lot. Everybody play soccer in China."

Emily stops and takes a deep breath, "How did you hurt your leg?"

Ming says, "Long story, I make short. Father and I go hike in mountain area near home in China. Father look for herbs to make medicine. It was time before winter. Little chilly. No snow, but ice. We take new path that we not walk before. We get to narrow ledge we must cross or go back. Father cross first—easily—he have good balance. I start to cross. He say, 'Don't look down.' But of course, I look down. I see it very steep and far down another cliff. I should not look down. When I did, I get scared and lose balance. I fall and start sliding down mountain. I try grab branch and small trees but no good. They break off—I sliding fast. I see cliff coming. Big drop. Far down. I see two big boulders there. I going right for them. I think I will go over cliff. Suddenly I slide into boulder. My left leg get caught and I hear loud CRACK!"

"Oh, no!" exclaims Emily.

"Oh, yeah. Big pain. I start cry, 'Father! Father!' He sliding down to me. I hear him call, 'I coming, I coming! Don't worry!' He get to me and hold me long time. I love him so much."

Emily says, "I can see that. He is a very wonderful and gentle man."

Ming continues, "Very slow he pull leg free and lift me on his back. He carry me all way back up hill. Not easy I know. He never said word."

Emily and Ming continue down the path to Ming's home. It is getting darker now, but their eyes have adjusted so they can see the path. Emily asks, "Did you break your leg?"

"Yes," says Ming.

"Did he take you to the hospital?"

"Yes. Doctors say, 'Very bad break, maybe lose leg.' Father say, 'No. No. No lose leg.' They put me in cast, and Father take me home in wheelchair."

"Wow, that is so sad," says Emily.

"Father take care of me. He acupuncturist."

"Oh, yeah, I heard of that. They use needles, right?"

"Yes, small needle and other things too. He work on me six months and leg heal pretty good. I always have limp but also I always have leg."

"I'm so glad. Your father must be a good doctor."

"Yes, very good doctor. He help lot of people. My grandfather acupuncturist too. House around bend."

Ming continues to brace Emily with her shoulder; they look

like two soldiers returning home from battle victorious. Soon they come upon a beautiful two-story colonial style home with candle lights in each window.

"Oh look, Emily. There our house. Lights on. Father home." Ming helps Emily up the few steps to the front door and rings the bell. "Are you ok, Emily?"

"Yes, I'm ok, *Sh-yea Sh-yea*. This is a beautiful house, Ming, and the candles in the windows are magical."

"My Father love to turn on electric candles every night and come out to look at house and say, 'Our home say welcome.'"

"Yes, it really feels like that. It is so peaceful here with the tall trees."

Then, the front door opens slowly. Dr. Yang stands in the open doorway and, with a big smile, he says, "Welcome ladies, and a special welcome to our first guest. Hello, Emily, *Huangying*, welcome."

"*Xie Xie*, Dr. Yang."

"Oh, you've started to learn Chinese, Emily. Very good, your pronunciation is excellent."

"*Xie Xie* Dr. Yang. Your house is beautiful, and I love the lights in the windows."

"Yes, we believe it brings our home to life."

"It feels like that," says Emily.

INSIDE MING'S HOME

Dr. Yang holds the door open, "Welcome to our simple dwelling, Emily."

"Thank you," says Emily as Ming helps her into the house. Dr. Yang notices how Emily is limping.

"What happen here?" Dr. Yang asks seriously.

"Emily trip in dark over dumb, stupid log."

"I've never met a dumb, stupid log," says Dr. Yang.

"And I don't think you want to either, Father."

"Well, shall we take a look at the injury in a few minutes?"

"Oh, I think I'll be ok. I don't want to bother you," says Emily gritting her teeth. Changing the subject, she says, "Your home is so beautiful. There are so many pretty things, I'd love to take a look around."

"Sure," says Ming. "We'll take you on tour."

They all continue moving through the house. Emily looks around as if she is in a museum. She notices a photograph hanging on the wall of a soccer player performing a bicycle kick in midair. With rapt attention she says, "Wow! Who is that doing a bicycle kick?"

"Oh, a member of family," answers Dr. Yang.

"He must be really good to do that perfect a bicycle kick!" says Emily.

"He could be impressive in his day...like many soccer players."

"I bet he won a lot of soccer matches with his talent," says Emily.

"You may not know this at your age, Emily, but when you get older and have played a lot of soccer, this story may mean more to you. It's a story about—when winning is losing."

"How can winning be losing?"

"Just listen. I knew this man very well. He was an excellent soccer player. He had won many trophies, and his team had won numerous championships. He was an excellent dribbler and could

44

excite the crowd with his bicycle kick. When he was older and did not play soccer anymore, he vacationed in a remote area of China. He came upon a recreational area where children were playing basketball, tennis and other sports. There was even a small soccer field. Watching the children play the different sports in those fields, memories of his own childhood swam through his mind. Suddenly, a soccer ball came rolling up to his feet. In a spontaneous reaction, he put his foot on the ball and started moving it around—rolling it up to the top of his foot, then tapping it to his knee, then tapping it from one knee to the other knee, then tapping it up to his back and letting it roll down his back, and then kicking it up over his head with the back of his heel in a perfect rainbow kick. He started dribbling with the ball, and then he looked up and saw a teenage boy about 19 years old approaching. He said to him, 'Oh, sorry. Is this your soccer ball?'

'Yes,' the boy said. 'You seem to be a friend to the soccer ball.'

'Yes,' the man said, 'I spent many hours together with a soccer ball as a youth.'

'You have some good moves,' the boy said.

'Thank you, said the man, 'But I'm afraid I'm pretty rusty.'

'Would you like to play some one-on-one with me—maybe a game up to 15 goals?

The man felt a little nervous but said, 'Sure why not. Do you enjoy beating old men at sports?

'I don't think it's going to be so easy to beat you.'

'Oh, you'll be surprised,' the man smiled."

Dr. Yang continued, "So the game started, and it was pretty even up to the end when my friend went ahead 14 to 13. Then he told me, 'The boy kicked a beautiful long shot that was completely out of my reach.' The score was tied 14 to 14. My friend got the ball and he started wondering, 'Can I beat this young fellow? I have to prove to myself that I can still play. I can hear the fans cheering me on. I have to go for it. It may hurt the boy's feelings, but I have to prove to myself that I'm still a great soccer player.'

"So, he remembers a play that never failed him. It entailed some very fancy dribbling—moving the ball back and forth, faking with the body left and then passing the ball behind his own back to the right, getting a step in front of the other player and then driving it into the net. But then, he started feeling some compassion for this young boy. Many thoughts start racing through his mind, 'How is this young boy going to feel getting beaten by an older man who hasn't played in years? Should I use this killer stroke that has never failed me? Or should I let the boy steal the ball from me and make the winning goal? Then he'll feel good about himself. On the other hand, it's the perfect opportunity to show myself and him that I've still got the stuff of a great player. I think I can beat him. He's a good player. He's lost at soccer before. Nobody wins every game. I didn't ask him to play a game...he asked me. So, I'm sure he had the feeling he could easily beat an old man. 'What should I do? What should I do? Lose or win?' Then he decides. 'I'm going for the killer stroke. I have to do it. I have to prove to myself that I can do it—that I've still got it. Yes, I'll go for it.' He does some fancy dribbling and then goes in for the kill. He gets close to the boy. He fakes to the left. The boy goes for the fake. The man steps over the ball, and, first with his right foot and then with his left, kicks the ball behind his back. The boy tries for the steal, loses his balance and can't find the ball. Then, suddenly, the man shoots a nutmeg between the boy's legs. The man runs behind the boy, retrieves the ball, and kills it into the net. He raises his arms and jumps in the air as he did many years ago and feels the spirit of his fellow players jumping on him in congratulations. When he catches his breath, he looks over to the young man. The boy is distraught. He picks up his soccer ball as if it weighs fifty pounds. He starts to walk away. The older man runs up to him and holds out his hand to get a handshake. He says to the young man, 'Thanks for the great game. You're really a good player.'

'Yeah, but not good enough, right?'

'I just got lucky. Let's shake on it.

'Right,' says the boy sadly."

As the man shook the young fellow's hand, he could feel instantly that he had done the wrong thing. The young fellow walked away with the weight of a lifetime on his shoulders, full of sorrow and self-anger.

"My friend told me that this moment has stayed with him all his life. 'It haunts me,' he told me. 'It keeps coming back and I can't get it out of my mind. When I made the decision to go for the killer shot, I knew it was wrong. It was my ego. You know why it hurts so much?' he asked me. 'No, I don't,' I said.

'It hurts so terribly, because I can't make it right. I can't do it over and make it right; let the young man win, get some joy and confidence in himself, and then tell his friends how he won the game. Instead I had to feed my old man's ego.' My friend kept repeating to himself, 'Worthless, worthless, shame.'

"This is the story my friend told me," Dr. Yang said. "Please remember this story as you go through life. I was very close to him, so I could feel his hurt within myself."

"That was a sad story," said Emily.

"Yes, it was a true story, and I told it to you because you are sensitive and perceptive and it may prove to be an asset—a benefit in your life that will save you from much grief."

"Thank you, sir. I don't quite understand everything about it, but the way you told the story, I could feel what you were going through and what the young man was going through. I will never forget that story. Thank you."

"On the other hand, Emily, I have a story for you that I call: 'When losing is winning.'"

"Oh, no! How can losing be winning?"

"It sounds crazy, but it's a true story, and it's a very happy story. Ming and I were present to witness it and I'll tell it to you some day."

"When?"

"When the time is right. And when that time comes, we'll know. I guarantee it."

"Ok, Dr. Yang, I'll take your word for it."

Emily stops at another framed photograph of a young girl doing a butterfly kick. Emily gets up close to it and exclaims. "Ming! Is that you? Ming! That's you, isn't it? Doing a butterfly kick! Wow, that's terrific!"

"That's Ming alright," says Dr. Yang proudly. "That's my Ming!"

Emily is very excited. "You're really good Ming. It looks like you're flying!"

"Sometimes feels like that too," answers Ming.

"Emily, there's an ancient teaching in China called, *Udhama*," says Dr. Yang. "*Udhama* is a part of martial arts in China. Maybe you have seen the movie, *Crouching Tiger Hidden Dragon*. They perform *Udhama* in that movie, fighting with swords up in the trees.

But I think it was mostly done with wires attached to the actors." He laughs. "It is practiced to allow one to become extraordinarily buoyant– able to leap up to great heights, to feel as if suspended in air, to feel light as a feather—going beyond normal physical possibilities. We've seen people who are quite proficient with it."

Emily asks, "Can you teach me?"

"You have to study with a master for a long time," says Dr. Yang. "You would have to go China. I can show you a little. I learned some when I was young and playing soccer. I can show you acupuncture points you can rub that will help you become more buoyant, stronger, feel lighter, and feel like you're floating."

"Which ones are they?"

"I'll show you later, Emily. They are very common points but today most people are too busy to practice them or aren't disciplined enough to take the time to achieve even a little bit of *Udhama*."

"Thank you so much, Dr. Yang. Everything is so beautiful in your house and there's a very peaceful feeling too."

"Thank you, Emily," says Dr. Yang.

They continue walking through the home. Emily stops in front of a beautiful silk wall hanging painted in ink with Chinese letters in ancient calligraphy. "Oh, look at this," smiles Emily, "I love this! These letters look like they're dancing on the silk."

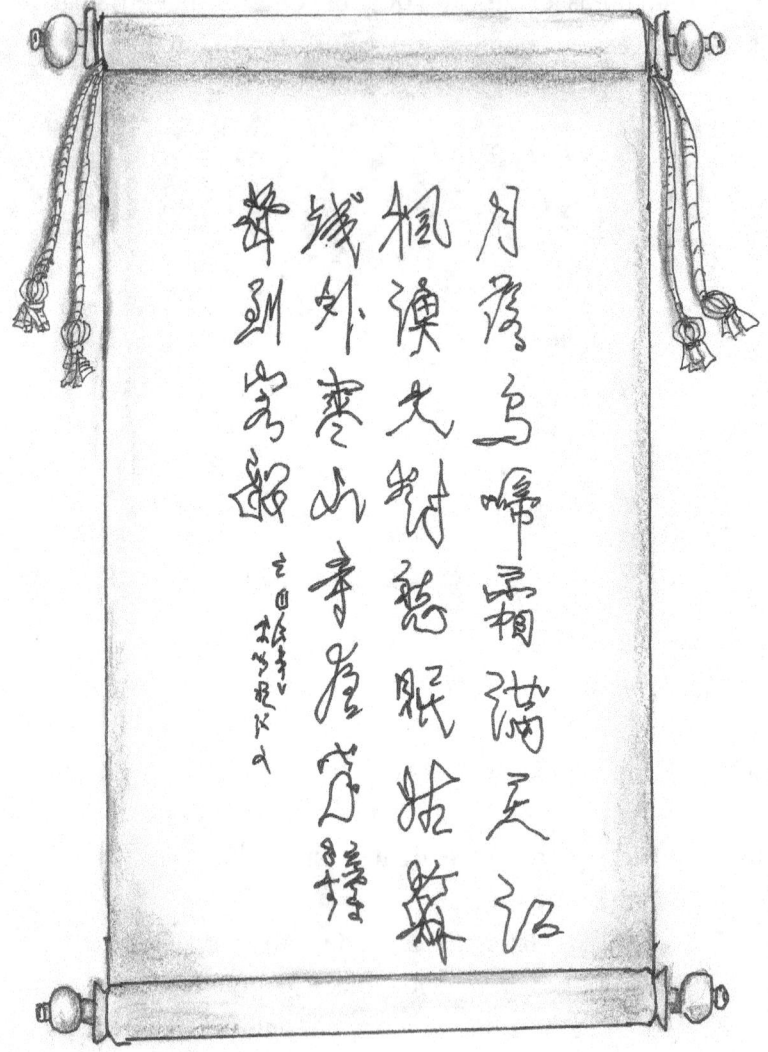

"Emily sees dancing in everything, Father."

"Does she see dancing in soccer?"

Emily scratches her head. "I never thought of it, Dr. Yang. But I guess I could see dancing in soccer, if I thought about it for a little while. Yes, the way we move and turn. Sometimes it becomes a pretty rough dance I'm afraid." They all laugh. "But what do all these letters say on this beautiful Chinese wall hanging?"

Dr. Yang starts to say, "Maybe Ming should tell it..."

Ming interrupts him. "No, you should tell Emily, Father. I love story so much. I could hear million times."

"Ok, Ming, just for our guest." Dr. Yang stands by the scroll and gestures to the letters as he speaks. "It is night-time in the woods. There is a lake in the valley. The full moon's white light reflects on the lake. A beautiful black bird flies out of the dark woods into the bright moonlight shining above the lake. This area of the woods is dangerous because men hunt birds with bows and arrows both day and night. There is a legend about the black bird. He flies out at night to gather moonlight on his wings and carries the moonlight back to the beautiful winged birds deep in the dark forest so they can see to gather their food. During the day men go into the woods to hunt these exotic, almost extinct birds. The hunters can get a lot of money for the beautiful feathers. The beautiful birds hide from the hunters during the day among the thick covering of the forest. At night, they look for their food with the light that the black bird brings to them on his wings. It would be very auspicious, very rewarding for the hunter who could bring down that courageous black bird. It would make the hunter very famous in the eyes of the other hunters in that region, and the hunters would become very rich because they would be able to hunt all the other birds for their beautiful feathers. The black bird in this story is very brave...flying out into the moon light is a very courageous sacrifice night after night. He was full of compassion for his fellow birds. Do you know this word 'compassion,' Emily?"

"I think it means loving."

"Very good, Emily. You are very smart just like Ming. No wonder you are good friends."

"Dr. Yang, your home is like a museum."

"Thank you, Emily. Ming helped me pick out many of the statues of Buddha you see."

"Come here into special room, Emily," says Ming. Ming ushers Emily into a small room off the main hallway.

Emily, gasps at what she sees. It is a tall five-foot statue of a beautiful Chinese woman who is dressed in warrior gear. Emily becomes mesmerized by the beauty of the statue. "Who is she? She looks almost real. She is so beautiful."

"Tell her, Father," says Ming.

"You can tell her, Ming. You know the story very well."

"Thank you, Father," she smiles and turns to her friend, "Emily, her name *Quan Yin*. In China, *Quan Yin* is Goddess of Compassion, Mercy and Kindness. Her full name *Quan-she Yin* which mean, 'She who hears cries of suffering in world.'"

"Just looking at her makes me feel so peaceful," says Emily continuing to stare at the statue.

Dr. Yang adds, "There are many ways artists portray *Quan Yin*, Emily. Sometimes we see her in a very dignified manner standing tall with long flowing robes. In other ways, like this one, as a warrior at rest after battling the evils that cause suffering in this world. She is said to manifest wherever there is suffering, and human beings need help. Acupuncturists have adopted her as their symbol of health, healing and compassion."

"I could stay here and look at her for hours," says Emily.

"We know what you mean, Emily," says Dr. Yang. "But since *Quan Yin* has put you in a much more relaxed mood, do you think I could have a quick look at your knee?"

"Oh, yes, sure Dr. Yang. I think that would be fine." Says Emily in a more amenable manner. "But I don't want any needles."

"Oh, you don't have to have any needles, Emily, if you don't want them," says Dr. Yang.

"Don't want them, sir."

"Fine. Now let's have a seat and take a look. But first I must wash some of this dirt off. These soccer pants don't give you much protection when it comes to dumb, stupid logs."

The Doctor examines Emily's right knee area. Emily asks sheepishly, "I have a soccer game this weekend. It's very important. It's the tournament game. If we win, we're the champs!"

"Oh, that's great," says Doctor Yang. "I'm going to palpate... press on a few spots and you tell me if they're sore, ok?"

"Ok...oh yeah that place is pretty sore... and that one too. Do you think my knee will be ok?"

"It depends?" says the Doctor.

"On what?" asks Emily.

"On you, Emily! Right Father?" interjects Ming.

"That's right, Ming," her Father answers.

Emily looks worried. "But...but...ah...on me? What does that mean?"

Ming says, "Emily you remember the story I told you about

falling down the mountain?"

"Yes."

"Well, if you let father work on you, you have better chance to play this weekend and be in really good shape. Right, Father?"

"Let me explain something to you, Emily," says Dr. Yang compassionately.

"Do you have to use needles?" Emily asks again with a quivering voice.

"I could use my fingers for acupressure, but the points I want to use are too far apart for me to reach and hold for 15 minutes. Ming, please get me a box of *Seirin* needles with the red handles."

"Ok, Father." Ming goes to a cabinet, opens it, and brings out a small red box and hands it to her father. He opens the box and takes out a small package. He opens the package and takes out a small acupuncture needle about two inches long including its red handle.

Emily says, "Oh, they're very small."

"These are the finest acupuncture needles in the world, Emily. They're from Japan."

"You can barely feel them, Emily," consoles Ming.

"Do you put some medicine on the needles, Doctor?"

"No, Emily. No medicine."

"What do they do? Do they go in deep?"

"No, they go in very shallow, Emily. You see there are basically three things the needle accomplishes. Number one, when the acupuncture needle goes in, more red and white blood cells come to the area. That starts the healing process. Number two...Ming please bring the acupuncture man."

Emily ask with surprise, "There's an acupuncture man here?"

Ming and her father laugh, as Ming brings in a rubber statue about 20 inches tall with all the acupuncture channels drawn on his body. The doctor explains to Emily. "You see all these lines, Emily? And the little numbers everywhere? Well, the lines are the meridians or the energy pathways in our bodies, and the little numbers are the names of the acupuncture points where the needles go. You see the spot here where your knee hurts? This is the Stomach Channel. It starts right under your eye and it goes all the way down past your knee to your second toe."

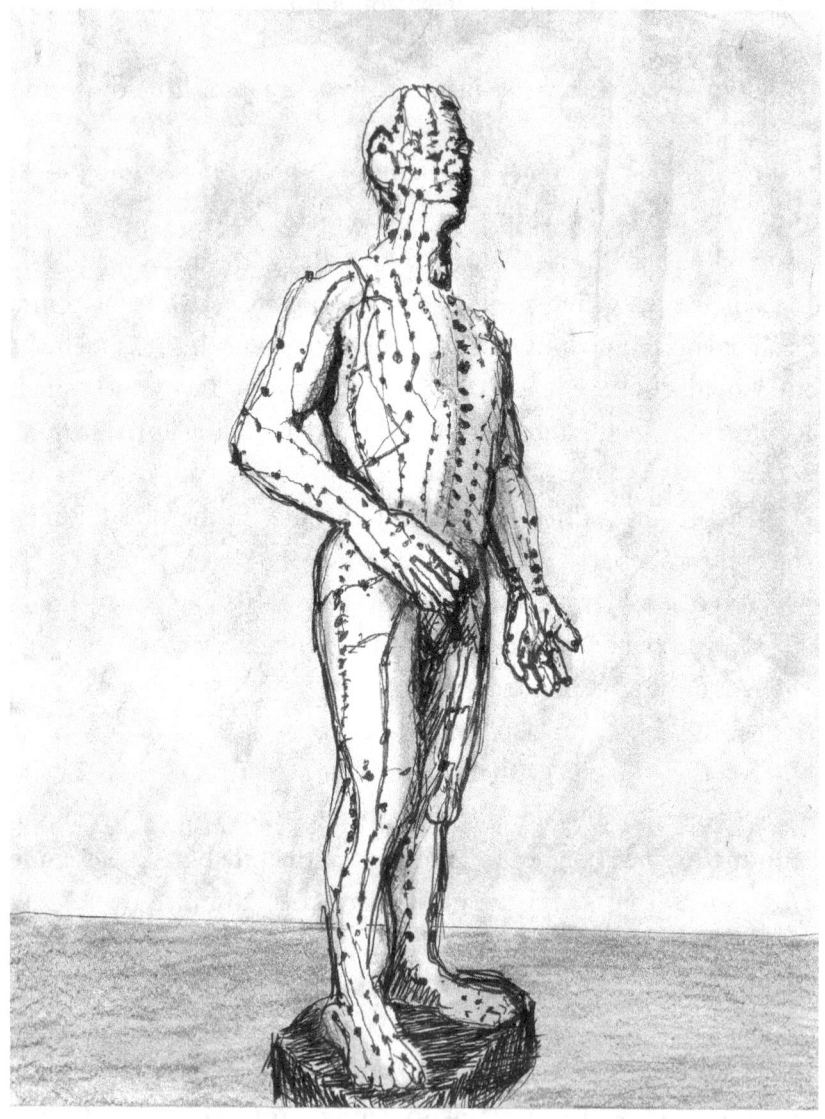

"Is there something wrong with my stomach?" asks Emily.

The doctor smiles, "No, Emily this is how the energy of the

stomach channel flows: from the eye, down to the toe. When the needle goes in, very shallowly of course, more red and white blood cells come to the area. Also, the needle starts the energy moving in the channel, and it breaks up any stagnation or stuck blood in that channel. You know how something gets black and blue when you get a bruise? That's because the blood is stuck there. We want to get that blood moving so the pain will stop. Then the final thing that happens is this: when the needle goes into the acupuncture point, the brain doesn't say, 'Oh, whoopee! We're going to have acupuncture!' No. The brain says, 'Oh, foreign object in the body! Send out the pain killers!' The pain killers of the brain are called Beta Endorphins which help take away the pain. What we have done is fool the brain. We put in the needle to help the body, and the brain thinks it's a bad thing and sends out the pain killers. But the pain killers don't affect the needle, the pain killers kill the pain and make you feel calm."

"Do the needles hurt?" asks Emily with a trembling voice.

"Come here, Ming. Sit down and roll up your trousers past your knee." Ming sits down and rolls up her trousers. The doctor takes out the acupuncture needle. "Now, Emily, with this cotton ball, dampened with alcohol, I'm going to wipe the area where I will place the needle." He wipes the area below the knee cap. "You see, Emily there's a little guide tube that is a little shorter than the needle. We tap the handle, and the needle goes in very quickly. Are you ready Ming?"

"Ready, Father." The doctor taps in the needle.

Emily, with eyes wide open, looks at Ming. "Are you ok, Ming?"

"I fine. Just felt tiny pinch that gone in a second. Sometimes feel nothing. Easier than falling off log! If you get drift... as Americans say. Want to try?"

"I don't know."

Ming looks at Emily and asks her seriously, "Emily do you want to win that soccer game this weekend?"

"Yes! You know I do!"

"If you don't let Father help you...you might be sitting on bench."

Dr. Yang speaks seriously to Emily, "Emily, I know you are a very intelligent, talented and courageous young lady and I want to prove this to you."

"How can you do that, Dr. Yang?"

"You must have heard of astrology. It is a study where you can find out many beautiful things about yourself—what kind of person you are, for example, which can help you get through all kinds of situations in life, big and small. If you want me to look up your chart for you, just tell me when your birthday is."

"Yes, please. June 1st, 2008."

"Ok, fine. Ming, please bring our laptop computer in here. Now, Emily Chinese astrology is a very ancient study. It is true. It isn't something made up in a computer game. It's not a game. You can look it up yourself on your computer when you get home."

Dr. Yang opens his computer and gets to the correct site. "In Chinese astrology, we are compared to animals. We can be horses, sheep, dogs, dragons, rabbits, or tigers. There are 12 animals you could be." Dr. Yang studies the computer screen. "In Chinese Astrology, Emily, you are a rabbit."

Ming gets very excited. "Oh, rabbit. I love rabbit! I glad you a rabbit. I rabbit too. Maybe we can eat carrot together later."

"Yeah, like Bugs Bunny," Emily chuckles. And then both girls giggle.

"Yes, girls, and rabbit is a joyful sign as well." says Dr. Yang, "Now, I'll read to you more fully what kind of person a rabbit is. First, she is a steady person—she is a person that doesn't get flustered easily. You see you didn't get too flustered when you tripped over that dumb, stupid log."

"Maybe just a little," says Emily.

"Very, very little, Father," interjects Ming.

"The rabbit is an elegant person," reads Dr. Yang.

Ming says, "Emily is such a beautiful dancer."

"The rabbit is a sophisticated person," Dr. Yang looks at Emily.

"Oh, yes." says, Ming. "When Emily walks in a room everyone looks at her and sighs and thinks how sophisticated she is even for a young girl."

Dr. Yang continues, "The rabbit suggests a peaceful person, very loving."

"Of course, you can tell by the way she treats Pegasus and Fritz," says Ming.

Dr. Yang reads on. "She gets respect in a friendship or social group."

"Oh, yes," says Ming. "The whole Amigo Soccer team loves and respects Emily so much."

"The rabbit can easily make new friends," says Dr. Yang. Ming and Emily hug each other with a lot of laughter. "This is a nice one," says Dr. Yang. "She easily manages to make others happy."

"Oh, yes," says Ming, "I'm so happy when I'm around Emily."

"She is a peacemaker" Dr. Yang, says and continues, "Oh, that is *very* good. We need peacemakers, especially in today's world."

"Oh, yes," says Ming, "Even in Cincinnati...I'm sure."

"Ok," says Dr. Yang "She has good communication skills. She can teach people in a kind and gentle way. I'm sure she can do that," he adds.

Emily interjects, "Maybe I can do that because my grandfather, Bibou, and my grandmother, Kay-Kay, are such good Montessori school teachers."

Dr. Yang exclaims happily. "Oh, that's so good. I know of Montessori schools in Shanghai and Beijing, China. I have friends that send their children there. They say the Montessori schools are excellent."

Dr. Yang continues reading, "The rabbit has good diplomatic skills. She doesn't take sides in a fight, but instead helps others to resolve their differences."

Emily thinks aloud, "Maybe I need to work on that one a little harder." Ming chuckles.

"And finally…" says, Dr. Yang…

Ming interrupts, "Oh, let me read last one, Father. May I?"

"Sure Ming, go ahead."

Ming reads very softly and sweetly, "People love to be around her because she is so generous. That's right, Emily is so generous with all she has, especially her loving kindness."

"Boy, that was really wonderful," says Emily. "I hope I can live up to all those excellent qualities. Now I'm ready for anything. Ok. Let's do some acupuncture, Dr. Yang!"

"There's just one thing we have to do first, Emily," says Dr. Yang. "Oh…uh…what's that?" asks Emily cautiously. "We have to call your mother and get her permission."

"Oh, really? She won't mind."

"It's the law, Emily," says Dr. Yang seriously.

"Oh…the law, well…ok…I guess." Emily says reluctantly.

"Get my cell phone, please, Ming," requests Dr. Yang.

Ming moves quickly out of the room and comes back with a cell phone. "Here, Emily," says Ming. "Please call your mother."

Emily presses the numbers and listens for the ring. "I'll take it Emily," says Dr. Yang. "I'll put it on speaker."

A woman's voice answer on the phone. "Hello, Hall's residence."

"Dr. Hall, this is Dr. Yang. I'm an acupuncturist from China."

"Oh, Dr. Yang. I met you for a few minutes the other day at the hospital. I'm an anesthesiologist, and I was just going into the operating room. I remember saying hello to you. You're the friend of Dr. Liang, right? He was telling us all about you before you came to America, and we were so happy to finally meet you."

"Oh yes, I remember you now. Very nice to have met you."

"Thank you. How can I help you? And… how did you get my number?"

"Your daughter Emily gave it to me."

"Emily? Is she there?"

"Yes, she is, by an interesting coincidence. My daughter, Ming and your daughter Emily have become good friends. Here Emily, say hello to your Mother."

Emily takes the phone sheepishly. "Hi, Mom..."

"Are you ok, Emily? We were worried about you."

"Oh, we were coming over to Ming's house after soccer practice and I tripped over a dumb, stupid log and scratched my knee. Uh... here talk to Dr. Yang."

"Hi, Dr. Hall. Emily and Ming were telling me that Emily tripped over this 'dumb, stupid log,' as they put it. So, I thought I would give Emily some Chinese first aid with some massage, heat application and maybe a few, maybe three or four tiny acupuncture needles. And, as you are aware, I had to call first to get permission from a parent."

"Well, Dr. Yang I think Emily is very fortunate to be in such kind and expert hands. If she wants to try acupuncture—I say go ahead. Would you like to try some acupuncture Emily? I've heard a lot of good things about it, and Dr. Yang, I've also been told, is the best."

"Sure, Mom, thanks. I think I'll give it a try. They have a really beautiful home. It's enchanting. I'll tell you about it later."

"Ok, good Emily. Love you. Have fun."

"Yeah, I guess. Love you too, Mom."

"Goodbye, Dr. Hall and don't worry, we'll drive Emily home after her treatment."

"Thank you very much, Dr. Yang. And again, welcome to America."

"Thank you, Dr. Hall it's really great to be here. The people have been so kind to us and make us feel welcome."

"We are the fortunate ones, Dr. Yang. I know Emily is in good hands. God bless you all."

"Goodbye, Dr. Hall." says Dr. Yang as he ends the call.

Emily sees Dr. Yang moving his hand above her knee up toward her head. "What are you doing, Dr. Yang?"

"I'm increasing the positive energy in your knee before I start working on it. Do you want to see how that works?"

"Yes."

"Ok, come over here, Ming. Hold your right arm straight out to the side, and Emily, you come here too. When I tell you, I want you to press Ming's arm toward the floor in a smooth steady motion without jerking her arm. Do you think you can do that?"

"I'll try."

"Good. I'll stand behind Ming so she can't see what I'm doing." Dr. Yang stands behind Ming and with his hand about 12 inches away from her body, he moves his hand from her lower back to the top of her head.

Emily puts her hand near Ming's wrist and presses down. "I can't move it. She's very strong."

"Ok, very good." Then Dr. Yang with his hand about 12 inches from her body washes the energy from the top of her head down to her low back. "Ok, Emily press Ming's arm down again."

Emily presses Ming's arm, and it goes down easily. "Wow, her arm went down so easily. What did you do?"

"I didn't do anything except deplete her energy. So now I will increase her energy again." Dr. Yang again swipes up her back. "Now try again Emily."

Emily presses on Ming's arm. "Wow, she's very strong again."

"This is a technique used in all kinds of sports like karate or wrestling."

"I wonder if you could do it in soccer?"

"Anything is possible, Emily. But you must always remember if you decrease an opponent's energy you must increase it again later, or it would be unhealthy for both of you."

"Why would it be unhealthy for a person if they didn't increase the energy after they weakened their opponent?"

"It's the law of nature, *as you sow, so shall you reap*. If you don't increase the opponent's energy again, something will more than likely happen that will weaken *your* energy. Safety first. Besides it's good sportsmanship and good sports-woman-ship to be courteous and considerate of your opponent—which is so very important."

"Ok, team, let's get busy. First things first. Ming, bring the *Zheng Gu Shi*."

"What's that?" asks Emily.

"It's something we rub on the area where there has been trauma or bruising. It's called 'Fix Bone Water'. It's used by all kinds of athletes in China, Kung Fu, Karate and of course Soccer."

Ming carries in a gallon jug filled with dark, reddish liquid.

"What's in that? That looks like a little snake in there! Is that a snake?" asks Emily.

Dr. Yang tries to soothe Emily. "There are many things in here Emily. There are snakes and scorpions, and sea creatures, and many, many herbs. Smell it. It smells good."

"Do I have to?"

"Watch me, Emily." Ming puts her nose near the opening of the gallon jug, takes a deep breath and with a big smile says, "Oh, wow! Scorpion! My favorite perfume!" Ming and Dr. Yang chuckle.

Emily smells it. "Actually, it does smells pretty good. How do you make it?"

"Well I don't think you'll make it on your own quite yet. It's a very ancient formula. What we do first is fill a gallon clay jug with Chinese wine. Then we put all these things in the jug, we bury it in the ground for six months, and then all the energies of the ingredients mix together and form a powerful..."

"Like the members of a soccer team..." Emily interrupts.

"Exactly. Very good, Emily." The Doctor agrees.

"Are you going to rub that on my knee?"

"Yes, if that's ok with you."

"Sure! I don't want to miss that soccer game."

The doctor pours some liquid in the palms of his hands, rubs them together and starts to massage around Emily's knee. He works it in for about five minutes. "That feels really good!" says Emily.

"Ok, Emily now we're going to use four needles. One in the knee, one in the elbow, one in the head, and one in the ear. Ok?"

"Ok! Doctor, you're the doctor." They all laugh.

"Before I insert the acupuncture needle, I will explain to you why I chose each point. The first point near the knee is called Stomach 36 or *ZuSanLi* it means 'Leg Three Miles.' It is the biggest qi and blood point of the body. That means it is the most energetic point of the body. It calls up the energy of the body to help with the healing. Before I insert the needle, I'll wipe the point with a cotton ball moistened with a little alcohol. When I say 'Ready' I want you to take a breath, and then when I say, 'Ok' I want you to blow it out with a little force. Understand?"

"Yes, sir."

Dr. Yang puts the guide tube with the needle near the outside of the knee cap. "Ready? Take a deep breath." And then after a few seconds he says, "Ok, let it out."

As Emily lets out her breath vigorously Dr. Yang inserts the needle. "That was fun. I didn't feel anything—maybe a tiny pinch!" says Emily courageously.

"Very good, Emily. The next point is Large Intestine 11 on the left elbow. Its name is *Quchi* or 'Pool at the Crook'. You see in Chinese Medicine we use reference points. If something is wrong in the foot, we treat the opposite hand. If something wrong with the knee we treat the opposite elbow. If something wrong with the shoulder, we treat the opposite hip. Get it?"

"Got it!" says Emily.

Dr. Yang places the needle near Emily's left elbow. "Ready, take a breath. Ok, let it out." Dr. Yang quickly inserts the needle. "How was that, Emily?"

"That was fun!"

"Good, the next point is Gall Bladder 16. Its name is, *Much-uang*—'Window of the Eye.' It's on the top of the head and also refers to the knee. Ready?"

Emily takes a deep breath. "Ok," says Dr. Yang, and Emily exhales. Dr. Yang inserts the needle. "Was that one ok, Emily?"

"I could feel it more than the others, but it wasn't bad. I don't feel anything now."

"Ok, good, Emily. You're really doing well for your first acupuncture treatment. I had the feeling you were a good candidate for acupuncture."

"Why?" asks Emily.

"Because you are fearless," says Dr. Yang.

"Like, *Quan Yin*?" asks Emily.

"Exactly, Emily. Just like *Quan Yin*."

"Emily?" says Ming. "I had a great idea. When you're 16 and you get a car, you can get a licensed plate with the letters, *Quan Yin*."

"Good idea, Ming, and you can get one that says, *Mai Wanti*." They all laugh.

"Ok, ladies, here comes the last needle. It goes in the ear."

"Oh, is this one going to hurt? None of the other ones have so far," exclaims Emily.

"I'll do my best, Emily. But you might feel a little pinch."

"Yeah," inserts Ming, "but it's nothing like getting kicked in shins by soccer opponent...guarantee!"

Emily laughs and says, "Ok, Dr. Yang, let's do it!"

"This ear point is also for the knee. Research and experience contend that the energy of the acupuncture points in the outer ear sends messages right to the brain, like 'fix my knee, please.'"

Emily, with a big smile. "Go for it, Doc! Fix my knee!"

"Ok, you ready?"

"Ready brain, here it comes!" Emily takes a deep breath.

"Ok," says Dr. Yang.

Emily exhales and Dr. Yang inserts his needle into the outer ear. "Beautiful!"

"Beautiful!" echoes Emily.

"Outstanding!" Ming joins in.

"Now Emily I'm going to warm each of the needles with a little moxa stick. Moxa is an herb that is lit and burns like coal. As you can see, it's shaped like a cigar to make it easy to handle. It is put near the acupuncture needle and sends heat down into the channel for healing. It is also very relaxing and soothing. How are you feeling?" Dr. Yang lights a candle and puts the moxa stick into the flame.

"I feel good. Actually, I feel a little sleepy. And, I love that moxa—the heat and the smell. I can feel the energy moving in my body. *Sh-yea Sh-yea*, Dr. Yang."

"*Mai wanti*, Emily. As I said, you're a good candidate for acupuncture because of your sensitivity—which also means you're going to have a quick and beneficial result from your treatment. Now Ming and I are going to sit here with you for 15 minutes. If you have any questions or discomfort, please don't hesitate to tell us."

"Dr. Yang, do you think acupuncture can help me play soccer better?"

"Well, Emily, it can't hurt." He chuckles, "Pardon the pun. Why do you ask?"

"Because sometimes I have trouble making goals."

Dr. Yang smiles, "Well, as all soccer players know, making goals is tough business. Now, there's one thing that helped me and also helped Ming. Maybe it can help you. Do you want to hear about it?"

"Oh, yes! A thousand times, *Yes!*"

"Ok. First, I'm going to ask you a few questions. Is that ok?"

"Absolutely," says Emily.

Ming jumps in with a chuckle. "Absorutry! as we say in China. Sorry folks, Chinese humor."

"Ok, Ming I'll let it slide this time. Now back to important business. Emily, you love your father and mother, don't you?"

"Yes, of course."

Dr. Yang continues, "And you love your horse and your dog."

"Yes."

"Do you ever think how much you love your soccer ball?"

"My soccer ball? No, I don't. I think it's a ball that gets kicked around a lot."

"Do you ever think about what the soccer ball is thinking?"

"Thinking? The soccer ball?"

"Do you ever think of the soccer ball as alive?"

"These are very interesting questions, Dr. Yang."

"Shall I go on?"

"Sure."

"Ok. In a way, everything is alive. Isn't it?" asks Dr. Yang.

"I don't know. Is it?" answers Emily.

"I think we might agree that to some degree everything is alive...like the earth, the trees, the rain, maybe even rocks. Is that possible for you?"

"I'll agree with that for now."

"Good girl. So, what we want to find out is—if you can consider, for this discussion, that it is possible that the soccer ball is alive to some degree. Can you go with that, or are you going to stick with the idea that the soccer ball is just a piece of leather and cloth filled with air...8.7 pounds per square inch, PSI as they call it?"

"I'll go with the suggestion that the soccer ball, for this discussion, is 'alive to some degree.'"

"Excellent!"

"Excellent!" echoes Ming.

Dr. Yang smiles, "Moving right along. Is there anything else, any *thing* else in your life that you love very much?"

"Yes."

"What would that be?"

"Do stuffed animals count?"

"I don't see why not. I think stuffed animals could count a lot in this discussion. What is your favorite stuffed animal?"

"I think my dog, Mickey?"

"You probably talk to him, yes?"

"Yes."

"Does Mickey talk back to you?"

Emily looks at Ming for a long moment and then looks at Dr.

Yang. "Yes, he talks back to me...silently."

"What does he say?" asks Dr. Yang.

Slightly embarrassed, Emily waits for a long time. Then Ming jumps in. "I know what he say. He say, 'I love you Emily because we friends. You take care of me. You brush me and sometimes you let me sleep with you and you won't let anything, or anybody hurt me!'"

"Is that true, Emily?" asks Dr. Yang.

"Yeah. I love him and he loves me."

"Do you ask him questions?"

"Yes."

"Does he answer you...I mean silently, as you say? You feel you can talk to him silently, yes?"

"Yes."

"Do you tell him secrets?"

"Yes."

"Tell me a secret you tell Mickey."

"I'm sorry, Dr. Yang. We can't tell anyone our secrets. We promised each other."

"You see. Mickey is just made of cloth and other things and yet you still communicate with him like he's alive, don't you?"

"Yes, I do."

"Well...maybe you could communicate with a soccer ball too. Don't you think?"

"I never thought of it. But people might laugh."

"You don't have to be embarrassed. Many people talk to inanimate objects. Athletes talk to basketballs, baseball bats, and tennis rackets. Grown men talk to their cars all the time. Especially older cars. If the car is going up a steep hill and having trouble making it, a man might say, 'Come on, Bessie. You can make it. Just a little bit farther, old girl.' And at the top of the hill he might say, 'Good girl, Bessie. I knew you could do it. I can always depend on you. And don't worry, I'm not going to trade you in and get one of those new fancy-shmancy ones like everybody else wants me to.' You see, it happens all the time, Emily."

"Yeah, I've heard boys talking to their bikes sometimes, especially before a race."

"Nobody is going to know," assures Dr. Yang. "It can be all done silently...mentally. Just for fun, what do you think a soccer ball is thinking during a game?"

"He wants to make a goal."

"Right! For whom?"

"Probably his friend."

"Who would be his friend?"

"The one that talks to him and treats him like a friend."

"Exactly!" says Dr. Yang. So, Emily, do you see what might be missing in your game?"

"Yes."

"What?"

"I have to make the soccer ball my friend and not treat him like he's just some piece of leather and cloth filled with air. I've got to wash him and polish him and talk to him."

"What's so special about friendships and the people we love?" asks Dr. Yang.

"I guess it's that we think of them a lot and hope they're ok and happy."

"Right. Why do we think of them a lot? Because we're connected to them. In some special way, they are part of us. They are connected to us. Do you feel connected to all the people and non-people we've talked about?"

"Yes," smiles Emily.

"Absolutely Emily. You're a very bright and sensitive person. You make teaching easy and enjoyable. I bet your teachers love having you in their classes."

"I love learning new things."

"Good. Now here's something you may not have heard of. Let

me tell you about how I learned about it. I had a scientist as a patient once. He was a very nice person and very intelligent. He could make complicated scientific theories easy to understand... even for me." Dr. Yang chuckles. "He told me about a theory in Physics, called *Measurement Theory*. He said the easiest way to understand it was to call it, the 'Theory of Attention.' I call it, 'The Theory of Connection.' This isn't just mood making, it is all proven by mathematical equations and experiments. The theory states that if you look at something or put your positive attention on it for a while you can change that object. You can even change an outcome of an event—or even change an object to have a positive influence on your own desire. That means if you are thinking positively about a soccer ball, your attention to that soccer ball will make that soccer ball work for you. If you think positively about that soccer ball, there's a better chance that soccer ball is going to go into the net the next time you kick for a goal. The only way you can see if this is true is to try it. But you must connect with that ball like we talked about...by being friends with the soccer ball you connect with him. Make him real."

Ming interjects, "Emily here's what helped me. I imagine that there are very thin, almost invisible wires connected to me and my Dad or me and the soccer ball. It could be like you're connected to your mom and dad or Pegasus or Mickey or the soccer ball. It just takes a few minutes a day thinking about it, and pretty soon you begin to feel it. I mean, I can feel it with you already. Do you feel something?"

"I can feel something. I thought it was friendship."

"Friendship! That it!" Ming happily acknowledges. "Friendship very strong 'connection;' like friendship you have with family, your animals and Mickey. Emily, if you do this with soccer ball, you will *feel* difference. You will *feel* connection. You *feel* 'wires' connected. Ball not separate from you. It *connected* to you. It part of you. Ball feel alive. It *is* alive. You see. When you watch YouTube, you see incredible soccer player dribbling down field—tremendous speed. You see their connection with ball...actually see and feel it. I know you can do it, Emily. You got what it take. It change your game. It change your life! Guarantee it! P.S. If you want me to, I be happy to help you with it!"

Emily shakes her head a few times as if to organize, classify and file all this overwhelming input. "How could I say, 'No' after that presentation?"

Dr. Yang looks at Emily in a diagnostic manner, "How are you feeling, Emily."

"A little loopy, actually."

"Good," smiles Dr. Yang.

"Actually, a little sleepy too," yawns Emily.

"Beta endorphin, right Father?" says Ming.

"Right, Ming."

"I feel numbness in my knee."

"Very good, Emily. The energy is working. We call that energy, *Qi*. You have good *Qi*, Emily. That is why you are an intelligent, good, natural athlete and why people like you."

Emily glances at Ming. "Well, maybe not everybody."

Dr. Yang smiles, "That's only because they don't know you very well. There is a special part of *qi* that is called, the *Shen* or Spirit. It is reflected in the face and eyes. People with good *Shen* have clear eyes, a beautiful smile and they just seem to shine like a bright sunny day. Their kindness is contagious. You have that, Emily. It is fortunate for you and for the people who get to know you. If you think there are people who don't like you, it's only because they haven't taken the time to know you. They are missing out on a great experience by not getting to know you."

"Thank you, Dr. Yang."

"Well, this has been a beautiful evening. I'm going to remove the acupuncture needles and then I think we better be getting you home."

"Can you show me those points for the floating procedure, Dr. Yang?"

"*Udhama*, sure. It will only take a minute. There are three. First one is right on top of the head. Du 20, *BaiHui* , 'Hundred Meetings'. I'll press on it with my fingernail. Feel it?"

"Yes."

"Second one is Stomach 36, the acupuncture point I did beneath your knee, *ZuSanLi*. 'Leg Three Miles'. Got it?"

"Yes."

"The last one is behind your back. You put your thumbs just below your rib cage in your lower back and press gently. That is Bladder 23, *ShenShu* 'Kidney Source'. A very important energy point for the kidneys where we get a lot of our energy. You can look them up on the internet."

"Thank you so much, Dr. Yang. I'll massage these points every day."

"Good, Emily."

"You be floating in no time, Emily," says Ming. They both laugh.

"Hey, Dad. You know, I had pretty rough day too. I could really use some acupuncture. And, I have to be ready for game also."

"Alright, Ming. Good idea. As soon as we've driven Emily home, I'll give you a treatment. I just received a new shipment of long, thick needles." They all laugh.

SOCCER PRACTICE THE DAY BEFORE THE TOURAMENT GAME

Coach Brady calls Ming over to him. "Ming, I've been watching you during practice. You seem to know your way pretty well around the soccer field. You're not only a really good soccer girl but you're a pretty good soccer player. You strike the ball power-fully and with consistent accuracy. Jenny has come down with the summer flu and won't be able to play tomorrow. I'd like you to take over her position on the Amigo soccer team. What do you say?"

"I say, it dream come true, Coach Brady. Thank you, thank you...*xie xie*."

"And *xie xie* to you, Ming."

Emily sees Ming talking to Coach Brady. She quickly goes over to the other Amigos and says, "It's the coach's birthday today. So, let's sing Happy Birthday to him like we practiced and tell him to take the afternoon off and go home to his party because I want to show you a new play that I learned. It's really cool."

Excitedly, they all agree. "Sounds great, Emily."

Emily and the Amigo team go over to Coach Brady. Emily tells him, "Coach we know it's your birthday and your wife told us she's having a party for you and she wants you home early. So we want to sing a special birthday song for you and then you better get home before they eat all your cake and ice cream."

"Ok, girls. A special song. Great! Let's hear it."

They all sing the Happy Birthday song:

"Happy Birthday to you Happy Tournament to you. We'll beat the Terrible Terminators Then we'll bring the trophy back to you."

The Coach with a big smile, "Thank you so much, Amigos. That was very nice of you. I have a really good feeling about this tournament. I know we're not the favorites to win, but I know we've got the courage and willpower to win. I'm looking forward to bringing that trophy to our trophy case."

Emily raises her hand. "I didn't know we had a trophy case, Coach?"

"Well, we'll have to get one made as soon as we win that trophy."

Very excited, Emily says, "I think we better have somebody start building that trophy case right now, Coach!"

All the Amigos cheer. "Happy Birthday Coach. Hip Hip Hooray."

"Why don't you have some practice shooting goals, and then you can go home early. I don't like parties much, but if I don't get home my wife is going to turn me into a soccer ball...if you know what I mean. Have a good practice and just think about having fun in this tournament game tomorrow. Take care."

The Amigo team watches the coach walk away. "Ok, Coach have a good time at your party."

When the coach is out of sight, Emily calls all the girls together. "Listen to this – my grandfather, Bibou, always has great ideas for soccer plays. He thought up a new one, and I think we can make it work if we get into a tight situation."

Her teammates urge her on. "Good idea, Emily, teach it to us."

"Ok," says Emily.

"It's called the 'Criss-Cross-Conundrum.'"

"What's a criss-cone under...whatever?" Brenda Jean asks.

"It's a Criss-Cross-Conundrum."

Veronica covers her mouth. "Emily! Isn't that a really bad word?"

"No! No! No! Veronica, 'conundrum' means 'confusion.' Bibou

never uses bad words. We do this to confuse the other team. So, it goes like this: I get about 20 feet from the goal and then you all start 'criss-crossing' back and forth in front of me so the other team can't get to me. I keep the ball protected. Then we start this rhythm. It's from one of Bibou's favorite songs by the band, 'Queen', called 'We Will Rock You.' We line up in a row in front of the ball. Then we go 'Boom Boom, CLAP' and clap our hands loudly. Clapping the hands is the sound of the Drum in Conun*drum*. Get it?

"So, it goes, 'Boom Boom, Clap', Boom Boom, Clap, Boom Boom, Clap', Boom Boom, Clap' We do this four times, and then we sing really loudly – 'We Will, We Will, Socc You, Clap Clap, Socc You, Clap Clap. We Will, We Will, Socc You, Clap Clap, Socc You, Clap Clap'. We do this two times and then here comes the really cool part. We are going to weaken the energy of the Terminators just for about a minute. We put our arms straight up in front of us and then rake then down real fast in the direction of the Terminators. Then real fast, everybody dives down flat on the field. The Terminators will be totally confused, and I do a 'rainbow' kick over my head to an Amigo teammate, and I'm out of the way, and she has a clear shot to the goal. I think it can work. I know it can work! It has to work! The thing is we've only got one chance. No one will probably ever see it again. But if we get a goal, we'll go down in Soccer History and so will Bibou. Can we do it, Amigos?"

"Yes, yes, yes!" The Amigos cheer.

"Ok, keep repeating this song in your minds from now on, and tomorrow we'll blow some minds! Let's go to bed early so we're all well rested." Then Emily shouts, "And no cokes!"

THE TOURNAMENT
DAY IS HERE!!!

Emily rides behind the bleachers on Pegasus, and behind her she holds the reins of a palomino mare. Fritz is close behind. Ming comes running up to Emily carrying some Amigo towels and bottles of water for the game.

"Hi, Emily. Hi, Pegasus. Hi, Fritz, and what a beautiful palomino."

"Did you ever ride a horse, Ming?" "Yes, Emily, before I walk, I ride horse." "Oh, that's great. Maybe you can show me some stuff," says Emily.

"What you mean?" asks Ming.

"I mean I brought this wonderful horse for you to ride after we beat those Terminators."

"Oh, thank you so much, Emily! She beautiful."

"Get on, Ming. Let's ride them around back of the shed and tie them up. Come on, Fritz!" Fritz barks in happiness and excitement.

Suddenly, Coach Brady comes running around the corner of the shed. "Emily! Ming! Where are the soccer balls? I can't find the soccer balls!"

"What, Coach? That can't be!" Emily and Ming exclaim in shock.

Ming almost starts crying, "Coach, I clean them all last night and I fill them this morning... careful with air...8.7 PSI!"

Emily calls, "Fritz, come on." Emily jumps off Pegasus and takes Fritz into the ball shed. "Find the balls, Fritz. Find the balls!" Fritz starts to bark and runs around in circles. Then putting his nose to the ground, he makes a break for the door. "Come on Ming. Come on Coach, let's follow Fritz!"

Emily and Ming get on Fritz's trail. Coach jumps on a nearby bicycle and tries to keep up. Fritz goes into a wooded area with thick brush and finds a dilapidated old shed. He starts barking loudly. Suddenly, Diesel and Grease stick their heads out of the old door. Emily exclaims "Diesel, Grease, do you have our soccer balls? What happened to these balls? They are all flat! What's wrong with you guys? We've got a tournament game this afternoon."

Then Coach comes huffing and puffing on his bicycle. "You found the balls! Good boy, Fritz! Good boy!" Coach notices the soccer balls. "My gosh! They're all flat." Coach is mad "Diesel... Grease...what's wrong with you guys? We'll deal with you later. Come on everybody, let's get these soccer balls back to the soccer field and get them prepared for the game. We've got to get 8.7 PSI into the balls right away. Diesel... Grease... you're coming with us to get these balls pumped up properly. After that, I'm going to call your father, Diesel, and see what we're going to do with you both."

"Don't tell my dad, Coach...please," pleads Diesel.

Grease pleads, "Yeah, Coach. We'll do anything you ask! My uncle is really strict!"

Coach Brady is serious. "We'll deal with you both later. We've got a soccer game to win and a little speed bump like this isn't going to stop us. Let's go everybody!"

They gather all the balls and take them to the locker room. Coach says, "Ok, you kids start inflating those soccer balls. Emily, Ming, you're in charge. If there's any more shenanigans you fellas are planning ... well, I don't think you want to get into any more trouble than you're in now...right fellas?"

"Right, Coach," they whimper, looking down at all the deflated soccer balls.

"Ok, then, get these soccer balls in shape."

Coach Brady turns around as he walks out the door. "I'll be back shortly and see how you're doing."

"Ok, let's get busy," orders Emily. "Diesel you work with me and Grease you work with Ming. Diesel, you're in charge of the pump and I'm in charge of making sure we're right on 8.7 PSI."

Diesel whines, "I wanna be in charge of the tire gauge. We work with tire gauges all the time with my dad."

Ming retorts, "Diesel, who Coach put in charge?"

Diesel concedes, "Ok, Ok!"

Emily says, "Why did you do such a thing as hide all the soccer balls and flatten them right before our big tournament game?"

"I'll tell you why!" comes a big voice from the locker room door.

Diesel yells, "DAD!!! What are you doin' here?"

"Uncle, Joe how did you get here so fast?"

"Like a lot of the Cincinnati soccer fans, I came to see a good team play soccer. I've been watching you guys all year and I want to see how winners play. Then got a call from Coach Brady. Why in Heaven's name did you deflate and hide all these soccer balls?"

"I don't know, Dad. Me and Grease thought it would be fun."

"Fun!" retorts Mr. Finerty. "This is embarrassing to me. I know why you did it. It's because you're jealous of this girls' soccer team. They won enough games that put them in the tournament finals and your team lost out in the first round."

"Ah...Dad. Our coach isn't any good and we got so many ball hogs that never pass..."

Mr. Finerty interrupts, "Yeah, Diesel and your real good at passin'...passin' the buck; makin' excuses why you don't win instead of going to practice all the time and workin' hard on your fundamentals like these girls. They could probably beat your team like a hot knife through butter."

Just then, Coach Brady makes an appearance at the Locker room doorway. "Glad to see you could make it so quickly, Mr. Finerty

Mr. Finerty greets Coach Brady with a handshake. "Hi Coach Brady, just call me, Joe."

"Girls?" asks Coach, "Did Joe tell you what Diesel and Grease have volunteered to do?"

"Volunteered?!" exclaim Diesel and Grease.

Emily and Ming say in unison, "No, Coach."

Diesel and Grease, also in unison, "We never volunteered for nuthin'!"

Joe says, "Yes you did, Buddy Boy. With my help!"

Grease and Diesel both say, "Volunteered for what?"

Joe says, "Making the Amigo soccer team a trophy case so they have a place to put the trophy that they're going to win this afternoon."

Emily and Ming jump with joy. "Yeah...a trophy case for our trophy. Thanks fellas!"

"We don't know how to build no trophy case," argue Diesel and Grease.

Emily gets very excited and says, "Now, everybody, look at me. Smile! And hold that pose!" Emily pantomimes like she is holding a camera and then she says, "'Click!' Please wait here. I've got a really, really big surprise for everyone. Please don't leave! I'll be right back."

They all watch Emily run out of the building.

Joe continues. "I know you don't know how to build a trophy case, but you'll learn how when I'm supervising the job

"Oh no! Uncle Joe...you're so strict..."

"Yeah, Grease...you better be careful. You might learn something."

"I'm sure you'll do a really good job fellas," says Coach Brady.

Ming happily jumps in, "Yeah, now I know sure we going to win trophy."

Diesel and Grease moan together..."Oh, brother!"

"Are all the soccer balls in good shape, Ming?" asks Coach.

"They perfect, Coach," says Ming.

Suddenly Emily pops into the room. Behind her is a tall good-looking blond-haired man with an impressive tan. "Everybody I'd like you to meet one of the best wood workers in fine finished furniture in the Cincinnati area, and oh yeah, he's also the rowing coach for the Cincinnati Junior Rowing Club and he coaches 500 high school kids in rowing. My dad, Steve Hall!"

Everyone is instantaneously excited! They all greet him at once. "High Mr. Hall. Nice to meet you."

Steve thanks everyone for their attention and says, "On the way back here, Emily was telling me you're going to build a trophy cabinet. That sounds great. I'd like to offer my services to help out if I can. I've got some really nice woodworking equipment in my shop and some extra lumber that might be of use."

"Wow, that's great, Steve." says Joe. "You're a gift from Heaven. Maybe we can get together after the game and talk about some plans."

"Sounds like a winner...just like the Amigos," says Steve.

Coach Brady adds, "Steve, we're so lucky to have Emily on our soccer team. She's an excellent player and an inspiration to the whole team." He claps his hands, "Ok, let's get out there and win us a soccer game!"

"Right on, Coach!" cheer Emily and Ming. As they all are leaving the locker room, Ming takes Emily's arm and whispers to her, "Emily what is a she-nancy-she-can?"

Emily chuckling to herself, "I'll tell you later, Ming." Emily and Ming go to change into their soccer gear.

Joe addresses Coach Brady. "Coach, is it ok if Diesel and Grease sit on the Amigo bench during the game?"

"Sure, Joe. That way they can help cheer on the Amigos but more importantly, we'll know where they are."

"Exactly my thoughts on the matter, Coach." Coach Brady waves goodbye as he walks out. "I've got to go over to the bleachers and greet some friends."

Joe Finerty puts his hands on the shoulders of Diesel and Grease, "Fellas I want to talk to you for a minute."

Diesel looks worried. "Oh no!"

"I don't want you two to move from this Amigo bench during the whole game, and I want you to show them your real and enthusiastic support! Got that?"

Diesel and Grease, "Yes, sir! Got it!"

Joe says to them. "Now come with me for a minute." Joe takes them behind the bleachers. He takes out a sheet of paper and his pen. He's talking intensely with them and writing things down. Diesel and Grease are laughing and excited about what they are talking about. Then Joe takes the paper, folds it in his pocket and leads the boys back to the Amigo bench.

Joe bends over between the boys and says in a low voice. "These are good people fellas. I want you to respect them and act your age."

Diesel says, "Dad I have to go to the bathroom. Is that ok?

Joe answers, "You get back here right away Diesel or I'm gonna come lookin' for ya. Got it?"

"Got it!" Diesel takes off running to the restrooms.

Grease looks at Joe seriously, "I thought we were acting our age, Uncle Joe."

Joe slaps his own forehead, "Yeah, unfortunately, I guess you were. Ok, no more horse'n around. The coach will be watching you both. I'll be back soon."

"Hey, Uncle Joe."

"What is it, Grease?" With a sense of sadness, Grease looks down to the ground.

Joe asks seriously, "Are you ok, Grease?"

"I'm ok, Uncle Joe. There's something I need to tell you. I've been carrying inside me for a long time."

"Well go ahead, Grease. Get it out. It's ok."

Grease looks up to his uncle, and with a tear in his eye he says, "I love you, Uncle Joe."

"Wow, Grease...thank you. I mean...you never said that before." Joe puts his hand on Grease's shoulder. What's up?"

"Nothin', felt like sayin' that now. I wanted to say it for a long time, but it never seemed to be the right time but today...I feel that this is a real special day like there's something like electricity in the air....the soccer tournament and everything. wanted to say thank you for takin' me in last year...well, you know when all that stuff happened with Mom and Dad."

"That's ok, Grease. You don't have to say anymore."

"I mean you took me into your family..."

"You are our family, Grease. Your dad was my brother. I loved him very much."

"I feel like you're my real dad now."

"I am Grease. I am."

"I felt this for a long time, but I thought maybe you might not like me and you'd put me in a foster home."

"We'd never do that. If we did that, we'd put Diesel in with you." They both chuckle.

"You're kiddin' right uncle Joe?"

"Just kiddin', Grease."

"You know what I feel like now, Uncle Joe?"

"What's that, Grease?

"I feel like an artificial flower."

"Really? What do you mean?"

"Well I went by the Salvation Army Store the other day and I saw these beautiful flowers in the window. I thought that I'd like to get them for Aunt Alice. I went in and asked the lady how much they were, and she said, 'They're a dollar, Sonny.' I asked her if she could put them on hold for me 'cause I was going to walk Mrs. Peacock's poodle for her since she's not feelin' so good, and Mrs. Peacock said she'd give me a $1.00 to walk it. I asked the Salvation lady if she'd keep'em in water, so they'd stay fresh till I came back with the dollar. She said, 'Oh, they'll stay fresh, Sonny. For a long, long time. They aren't real flowers. They're artificial flowers.' I said, 'They can't be! They look so real!' I went over and touched them and smelled them. They felt real soft and smelled good too. I said again, 'They look more real than real flowers!' 'Yeah, Sonny,' she said in a kinda sad way. 'Today, everywhere ya look, ya can't tell the artificial stuff from the real stuff. Makes ya wonder. Maybe someday it's all gonna be artificial stuff.' Then she looked out the window for a long time. 'Well, that's gonna be your problem, not mine. And, hey, you know what?'"

"Not yet?" I said.

"Keep your dollar. I'll make it up on somethin' else. There's a lot of rich folks comes in here. Which, I could never figure that one out. Ok, get out'a here before I change my mind. And hey, who you gonna give those flowers to?"

"My stepmom."

"Oh, she's gonna love'em. She's lucky to have a nice stepson like you. You're better than a lot of real sons. And, hey come back and see me sometime and tell me how she liked'em. Ok?"

"Ok. Thanks for give'n me the flowers."

"And then, Uncle Joe, as I was walk'in home I started to think. Hey, I'm like these artificial flowers. I'm not a real son. I'm an artificial son

"You're a real son to us, Grease."

"You treat me like a real son. I really love that. I guess like the lady said, some people probably can't really tell the difference."

"We couldn't ask for a better son who's such a good pal to Diesel. I'm sure your Aunt Alice is going to love those flowers."

"I hid 'em in my closet. I'll give them to her tomorrow for her birthday."

"You remembered her birthday. That's really good of you. She'll really appreciate that. Why don't you casually mention that later to Diesel, Ok?"

"Ok, Uncle Joe. Here comes Diesel now." Diesel comes over to Joe and Grease.

Joe says, "I gotta go and do what I have to do. You guys keep it a secret."

Diesel and Grease wave to Joe as he walks away. "See ya later, Dad."

"You guys root those Amigos to a victory, Ok?"

"Ok, we will!"

"Hey, Grease, what were you and Dad talkin' about?"

"Actin' our age."

"Yeah, I heard that one. What else?"

"We were talkin' about those real flowers over by the fence."

"Oh, those aren't real. They're fake flowers. I saw the janitor put those in the other day."

"How much you wanna bet, Diesel?"

"A quarter!"

"Ok, a quarter it is. Shake!" They shake hands and walk over to the flowers. They both bend over and touch them and smell them.

"Wow," says, Diesel. "They really are real. How did you know that?"

"Oh, when your dad and me were talkin' I thought I saw them kind'a turn our way and try to hear what we were talkin' about."

"Oh, yeah, right Grease. Hey, look the bleachers are really startin' to fill up."

SOCCER TOURNAMENT

The referee blows his whistle and says, "Ladies and Gentlemen welcome, the Amigo Soccer team from Cincinnati, Ohio and their coach, Larry Brady."

Loud cheering reverberates from the Amigo fans. "Go Amigos Go!" The Amigos wave to their fans as they run out on the field carrying their flag and doing some cartwheels. When the cheering settles down, the referee blows his whistle again and announces. "Soccer fans, I'd like to introduce the Terminators and their coach, Bob Burkhart from Toledo."

The Terminator fans start to cheer and whistle as the Terminator soccer team runs out on the field carrying a big black flag with a horrid skull painted in the middle and letters that look like they are dripping blood. They run around the perimeter of the field twice screaming and whooping like banshees, "Terminators! Terminators! We will terminate you! We will terminate you!"

The Amigo soccer team and their fans in the bleachers watch with open mouths in disbelief and confusion at the display by the Terminators. The Terminator coach goes to his side-lines smiling as he watches his girls' soccer team run excitedly around the perimeter of the soccer field.

Emily gets up and looks at her team. "Hey! Look at me! We didn't come here for a show-off parade! We came here to win a championship. None of these shenanigans are going to mean a hill of beans when we start racking up the goals. What-do-you-say? Let's get out there and bring home that trophy!"

"Right on, Emily! Right on!" They cheer.

Ming scratches her head and again whispers to herself, 'She-nancy-she-cans?"

Then Coach Brady watches as the referee walks over to talk with the Terminator coach. The referee shakes Coach Bob's hand and pats him on the shoulder, like old friends. Coach Brady looks down and shakes his head.

The referee and Terminator coach start a conversation. "Hi, Bob. How are ya?" asks the referee.

"Well...pretty good, Jerry," says Coach Bob sadly. "How's your son, Coach?"

"He's hangin' in there, Jerry. Like we all are. It was a tough pill to swallow after all those years of hard work and training and then having it end so abruptly. It was heart breaking."

"I'm glad you didn't give up coaching, Bob. You're the best. A little tough, I hear, but that's what's needed sometimes. We all know that, right? Hey, I saw where your Terminators won every game this season. This match is probably gonna be a walk in the park for your girls."

"Well, we'll see. We hope to make it a quick game. Maybe we'll give the Amigos an easy point, so they don't feel too bad," he says laughingly.

"You're such a sweet guy, Bob..." the referee chuckles sarcastically.

"It's a wonder the Amigos didn't forfeit the game out of fear when they heard they had to play your Terminators."

"We've been looking forward to this game. We've got one more space in our trophy case for this year's championship trophy and this one's a beauty. Hey listen, Jerry. Why don't you and your family come out to our cabin at the lake next week. We're havin' some friends over for a bar-b-que. We'd love to have you, Laura and the kids."

"Thanks, Bob. I know the kids and Laura love to come out to

your lake place. Thanks a lot. Well, it looks like it's time for 'Lambs to the Slaughter.'"

"Ref a good game, Jerry."

"You don't have to worry about that, Bob. Good luck...as if you need it."

The referee walks over to the Amigo bench. He puts his hand out to shake Coach Brady's hand. "Have a good game coach. Let's keep it clean."

"Yeah, Ref... clean, fair and square. Right?"

"Right, Coach. Fair and square," says the referee as he walks to the center of the field.

The game is about to start. The weather is perfect. The wind and the temperature are mild. The sun is overhead, so it won't be hampering either one of the teams' vision.

Coach Brady says to Veronica, "Veronica, you're the captain. So, if you have the choice to tell the referee which goal you want to defend, which will you choose?"

Veronica says, "Ming was telling me that her father always says defend the East because that's where the energy comes from as the world turns. What do you think Coach?"

"Let's get that energy workin' for us and go for it. East it is!" says the coach.

Both teams gather at the center of the field. The referee prepares to flip the coin. "Ok, Terminators, since you are the visiting team you call it...heads or tails."

"We choose Heads!" says, #13 the Terminator captain.

The referee flips the coin, and as it lands on the playing field, the referee and both captains bend down to examine the coin. The referee yells out, 'Tails!"

All the girls on the Amigo's team yell out, "East! East! East!"

"Well, I guess that settles it!" exclaims the referee as the shock of the girl's excitement rocks him back on his heels. He blows his whistle and makes an announcement. "This Tournament Soccer

Match will be played for 45 minutes with three 10-minute timeouts.

The Terminators are 'taking' the kickoff, and they kick to the Amigos. The Terminators kick off and the ball goes directly to Veronica. Veronica starts dribbling the ball down the field to the goal.

"Pass the ball, Veronica. Pass," shouts Coach Brady.

Veronica passes the ball to Brenda Jean who starts dribbling toward the Amigo goal. She is stumbling over herself. At about half-field she dribbles the ball too far out in front of herself, and, suddenly, #13 rushes in the path of Brenda Jean, steals the ball and with incredible power kicks the soccer ball with all her might, sending it very high above the playing field in the direction of the Terminator goal. It is so high that both teams and the fans lose sight of the ball in the brightness of the mid-day sun. Everyone is straining their necks to try to follow the trajectory of the soccer ball. They are all in a state of shock and awe.

Grease says to Diesel. "I've never seen anybody kick a soccer ball that high!"

Diesel analyzes, "She's probably got a metal plate in the toe of her shoe. I wouldn't put it past her."

#13 is ahead of both teams as she runs swiftly toward her goal. She looks up and can finally see her ball. She reaches her goal alone, with both teams running fast, trying to make up for lost time. Now it has come down to the Amigo goalie, Delores, and #13 face to face.

Delores is more than a little nervous. She takes a very deep breath and tries to put on her best 'game face.' She knows something big is going to happen but can't imagine what. Thoughts bounce through her head like a beehive struck by a soccer ball. 'Why did I want to be a goalie? I thought it was easy. You don't have to run all over the place. You can use your hands, and girls rarely even come close to making a goal. And now it's me and #13! Everybody's counting on me. I can feel it! Oh, God, please help me! Please!'

The soccer ball starts its descent. #13 is waiting for it about 20 feet from her goal. The ball dives like an Eagle about to land on its prey. With precise accuracy #13 catches the ball between her knees. She slides the ball down to her right foot. With gentle precision, she kicks the ball straight up about 4 feet over her head. When it descends just below shoulder height she bends to the left, lifts her right leg and kicks the soccer ball with tremendous power. It flies like a lightning bolt past the blank look on Delores' face. Delores, in disbelief, turns her head to the back of the goal and sees the ball stuck in the net. She then turns toward #13, who smiles at her broadly. Then Delores looks to Coach Brady who is trying to pull the hair out of both sides of his head. #13 runs high-stepping past the Amigo bench, "Gracias Amigos, gracias," and she laughs as she continues to her bench where all her teammates and Coach Bob are waiting to congratulate her.

The referee blows his whistle, "Goal! Terminators one, Amigos zero."

The Terminators kick off to the Amigos.

Emily picks up the ball and passes to Veronica. Veronica passes it back to Emily. The Amigos are getting closer to their goal. Emily passes to Ming. Ming passes to Veronica as she crosses in front of the goal.

Veronica's heart starts to beat faster. She thinks, 'I'm clear I'm clear. I've got a shot! I've got a shot!' Veronica takes a shot. It hits the side post and bounces about 10 feet from the goal. There is a big crowd around the ball. Emily gets the ball. Her back is to the goal. She takes a dribble a little farther away from the goal and then stops. She puts her right foot on top of the ball. She lowers her right foot and takes a step in front of the ball with her left foot, and in a few seconds visions flash through her mind of the ball moving through the crowd of players as if shot from a cannon. Without looking back to the goal, Emily does a powerful back kick with the heel of her shoe, and the ball magically and with tremendous speed passes though the crowded legs of both teams. Emily stops and does not look back at the goal. Then she hears the referee's whistle.

The referee shouts: "Goal—Amigos! Score—Terminators 1; Amigos 1."

Diesel punches Grease in the shoulder. "Hey, man! Did you see that? Emily did a 'Back-Door-Betty'! That's incredible! I've only seen Christiano Ronaldo and Lionel Messi do that!"

The Amigos and Coach Brady crowd around Emily, hugging her and hugging one another. "Wonderful shot, Emily. Incredible!"

Brenda Jean says, "It was beautiful, Emily!"

Ming asks, "How did you do that 'Back Door Betty', Emily?"

"I don't know. It just happened. I didn't think about it. I felt so connected to the ball. It just happened by itself. I knew the ball would find its way to the goal. I could feel the ball wanting to get to the goal somehow. I felt that I didn't do it. Something else did it. It was like an inner power took me over, and I was so calm, but I knew exactly what I was doing. It was magic. I never felt anything like that before!"

Veronica says softly, "Emily...can you teach me that kick sometime?"

Emily pretends she didn't hear Veronica and prepares for the kickoff. "Ok, team. We're back in the game. Defense! Defense!"

Veronica, very sad and angry pulls Emily to the side. "You know Emily, I should have made that goal; I tried. It was going straight for the goal. It's my fault. I should have made that goal... No! No! No! It's not my fault. It's my Dad's fault! I told him to get new balls and not these new stupid Amigo Jerseys. Those old balls don't kick straight. I tell you, Emily. If I don't make a goal this game, I'm never going to church again!"

Emily puts her hand on Veronica's shoulder. "Shake it off, Veronica. We're back in the game. We're a team. The Amigos are one unit. The team sets up the shot. It doesn't matter who kicks the goal. You'll get another chance. I guarantee it!"

"You guarantee it? Oh, Emily! Thank you, thank you! I needed to hear that. Golly, I sure could use a coke right now!"

"Easy Veronica...easy." Emily shakes her head.

The referee blows his whistle. The Amigos kick off to the Terminators. #9 secures the kickoff and passes to #13. Emily is right after #13. She stops her progress and backs her into a corner of the field. Then with a sweeping motion of her right foot she tries to steal the ball from #13. They get in close contact and struggle to get the ball, but neither one of them can free up the ball. Then the ball gets away from both. The ball goes directly to Ming. Ming has an open field and with great speed and dexterity, she dribbles the ball through the Terminators as if they were standing still. Finally, she has a clear chance to shoot a goal. She slams it. The ball is going directly to the goal. Suddenly, on its own, it seems to take off like a rocket. It changes its trajectory and hits the cross bar above the goalie. Ming kicked the ball so hard it rebounds to mid-field. #9 of the Terminators sees #13 near their goal with three Amigos all trying to prevent her from getting the ball. #9 kicks the ball hard and high. It is flying high in the air. The Amigos and #13 are waiting for it to come down. As it descends, they all jump for it trying to do a header and retrieve the ball, but #13, being taller than the others, jumps higher and does a skillful header into the net. She starts yelling in joy and running around the field at a triumphant pace with her knees bounding high like a drum majorette. The Terminator fans in the bleachers go ecstatic with joy and excitement, cheering their team and especially #13.

The referee blows his whistle and with a lot of enthusiasm yells out: "Terminators 2—Amigos 1!"

The Terminator coach huddles his team in real close. "Ok, we can't let down. We can't rest on our laurels. Remember what I told you about this Emily girl. We have to stop her. She's the real spark of that team. She makes things happen. We have to figure a way to stop her from taking over this game. Don't be so polite. This is soccer not a sleep-over party! Wake up!"

"We can do it, Coach!" says one of the Terminators.

"That's right! Now get out there and play like Terminators."

On the Amigo bench Emily and Ming are talking. "Ming, that #13 is pretty good."

"Pretty good?" exclaims Ming. "You serious? She is killer!"

"You're right. We have to block her off from possessing the ball so much. And we need a goal. We have to answer their points right away to break their confidence."

As Emily is talking, a beautiful Monarch butterfly flies around Ming's head and then lands gently on Ming's shoulder. Ming looks at the colorful Monarch and says, "Emily, it look like Mother Nature trying to tell us something."

"Right Ming. It looks like she says, 'Ming! It's time for your butterfly kick.'"

The Terminator goalie kicks off and sends a high, long kick deep into Amigo territory. Ming is there to receive the ball. She stops the ball with her lower right leg. She then starts dribbling the ball down the field. Emily crosses over to join her. Ming and Emily pass the ball back and forth going through the Terminator defense like Kewpie dolls at a state fair. They move the ball easily down field. Suddenly, Emily sees the Monarch butterfly circling around Ming's head. At this point, Ming continues to dribble and then shoots a hard, low kick to Emily. As the ball reaches Emily, she takes it more to the center of the field. Emily and Ming have reached a good distance to the goal, putting either of them in a good opportunity to kick for a goal. Then Emily dribbles the ball into a position to take a shot. As she approaches the ball, she jumps over the ball and kicks it behind her back. At this point, Ming starts spinning in the air as she did in the photo at her home and at the dance studio on the trampoline. The Terminators don't know what to expect of this.

Suddenly Bob, the Terminator coach, jumps up from his bench and starts screaming, "Watch out for the Butterfly! Watch out for the..."

At that moment, Emily turns toward Ming and fires a perfect pass with unbelievable accuracy, which reaches Ming at the exact moment her left leg can meet the ball.

The fans can see the intense concentration on Ming's face as she makes an incredible power kick toward the goal. But because of its fiery speed, it looks like the ball is going to overshoot the goal and land up in the bleachers. With fearful anxiety, the crowd stands up making loud sighs of 'Oh, No! Oh, No!' Then, as if blown by a strong wind, the ball makes a sudden turn to the right and enters past the goalie in the upper left corner of the goal, striking the net like it was going to burn a hole right through it. The Amigo fans jump up and down screaming with joy and almost breaking the bleachers in their enthusiasm, as all the Amigos run to Ming and shower her with hugs and "Great shot Ming! Beautiful Ming! Perfect Ming, perfect!"

The referee blows his whistle, "Terminators—2, Amigos—2"

Diesel and Grease are ecstatic; Diesel shouts, "Incredible butterfly by Ming! Perfect pass by Emily! The Amazing Amigos! One more goal! Bring home the trophy!"

Unable to control his enthusiasm, Fritz barks with joy!

Emily sees how happy Ming is and gives her two thumbs up. Ming smiles, and with both palms of her hands facing Emily, she locks her thumbs and then flaps her hands in an upward motion like a butterfly flying through the air. Emily blows her a kiss.

Ming looks up in the stands, finds her father, waves to him and then blows him a kiss. He returns the gesture two-fold.

At the Terminator bench, Coach Bob is throwing everything on the ground he can find. "She never should have made that butterfly kick. She should have never even had a chance to kick that butterfly. How could you let that Emily make such a perfect pass? Couldn't you read that? Didn't you hear me shouting from over here? You're playing like a bunch of little girls!"

In a sudden state of silent shock from their coach's remark, the Terminator girls take a quick glance at each other and then shake their heads like dogs—who have just come back inside out of a heavy rain.

Coach Bob continues, "You're giving this game away! Don't give those Amigos something they don't deserve. Get it in your heads, 'winning is everything!' When I say everything! I mean everything! Winning puts you on the top. Everybody wants to knock you off the top. No! Stay on the top. You haven't lost a game this year. Don't let this little Amigo... Shamigo...team take it away from you. Losing is not an option. Winning is the only answer."

Coach Bob starts to pace back and forth, "The road back from losing is too long...too hard. Believe me! You are winners! These Amigos are not winners! They're just having a little luck. You are winners. Take them down. Take them down now! No sympathy! No compassion! No tenderness!"

He takes a deep breath and points toward Emily. "Now look— see that girl Emily on the Amigos team? She's a winner. She's got winning in her veins. Can you see that? That's all she thinks about. I tell you because I know! She eats, drinks and sleeps winning! She's a champion! I see it in her eyes. She'll stop at nothing to win. Her blood boils with victory. She'll stop you anyway she can. She has no tenderness! No sympathy! No compassion! She'll take you down! Believe me! She'll take you down. We have to stop her. Yes! Yes! Yes!"

Beth, the smallest girl on the Terminator team raises her hand. "Coach Bob, how do you beat a person who never gives up?"

Coach Bob is losing his temper. "What kind of a...I'm not in the mood for any rhetorical questions, Beth."

Coach Bob turns around in a couple of circles and points to the end of the bench. "Beth, go sit on the end of the bench. I'm not going to have a coward playing on my team!"

Without much emotion, Beth gets up and calmly walks to a place at the end of the bench.

"Juanita, come here!" yells the coach,

From the end of the bench Juanita calls out with excitement. "Si, Coach Roberto!"

"What are you going to do when you get out there, Juanita?"

"*Detener senorita* Emily, Coach Roberto. Stop Emily! Stop Emily!"

"How do you feel, Juanita?"

"*Mucho valiente*! Very brave. No *temor*. No fear, Coach Roberto!"

"Good, Juanita. You know what has to be done."

"Si, Coach Roberto, *entiendo*. I understand."

"Good, can I count on you to stop that Emily?"

"*Si*, Coach Roberto. *Deja de* Emily. Stop Emily! *Primero*...but first Coach Roberto."

Coach Bob is getting more flustered with Juanita. "For cryin' out loud Juanita! Coach Bob! Call me Coach Bob!"

"Si, Coach Rober...Bob. I didn't realize I was calling you Coach Roberto. But...ah...I have one *pregunta*...one question...that is really bothering me."

Very frustrated, the coach asks, "Oh...come on...come on. "What is it, Juanita? What the *heck* is it?"

"What is a... what is a... please don't be mad...I can't think straight. I have to know. What is a...re...re...rhe...toric question?"

Coach Bob almost loses it. "Yieeee! Juanita go sit next to Beth! Juanita you're Hispanic! Maybe you should go play for the Amigos!" Coach Bob yells down to a heavy-set girl sitting at the end of the bench. "Lucy! Come here!" Lucy stands up. She is tall and husky. She pulls down her tight-fitting jersey that is more than a little too small for her. But it doesn't bother her now that she's finally getting to play for the Terminators. Her dream has come true.

"Are you ready to play Lucy?"

"Coach! I was born ready!"

"Ok, Lucy, you're the answer to our big problem and you're going to fix it for us." The Terminator Coach paces in front of his girls. "Team? is Soccer a contact sport?"

"Most definitely, Coach!"

The Terminators shout, "What kind of contacts are there? There are 3 types of contact in Soccer, Coach," they yell out. "1 — Legal Contact 2 — Accidental Contact 3 — Illegal contacts."

"What makes it illegal?" asks Coach Bob.

"Getting caught!" yell the Terminators.

"Tell me about the 3 types of contact in soccer, Lucy!"

"The first two are for sissies!" says Lucy.

"That's right, Lucy! Exactly right! Everybody does it. All the pros do it. Are you kidding me? They don't think they're playing people. They believe they're playing demons. Whatever it takes! That's their motto. Win! Win! Win! Whatever it takes. Right?"

The Terminators echo Coach Bob. "Absolutely right, Coach!"

Coach Bob draws his team in close to him. "Now come in here close and listen carefully to what I'm going to tell you. Lucy, we're going to use your talent."

"Thanks coach. I've waited a long time for this."

"I know you have, Lucy. This is going to be *your* day!"

"I was thinking something, Coach."

"Oh, no, no, no, Lucy. Not you too! What is it?"

With a wide smile on her face, Lucy says, "The Terminators are going to terminate.... Her!"

"That's right, Lucy but not so loud. People might misinterpret that. We don't really want to hurt anyone we just want to let them know who they're playing against!"

Lucy gets pumped, "She's playin' against the Terminators... Arrrgg!" Lucy gives Coach Bob a 'High Five.'

The Terminator team huddles in close to their Coach. Lucy

puts her arm across Coach Bob's shoulder. Coach Bob makes a lot of gestures with his hands moving left and right—up and down. Then with great gusto, Coach Bob yells out, "Now get out there and play like you're Terminators! - On 3!"

The team layers their hands and yells out, "One—Two—Three— Terminators!"

Beth and Juanita watch their fellow teammates rush out onto the field with great enthusiasm. Looking around, Juanita quietly asks Beth a question, "Beth? Do you know what a re-torkal..."

"Rhetorical question, Juanita?"

"Si."

"Well, a rhetorical question *sounds* like a question and it *looks* like a question on paper, but actually it *really isn't* a question."

"Why?"

"For two reasons, Juanita. One, because there's so many facets to the problem that there's really no simple answer to the question. And two, if there actually is one right answer—trying to find it would be like trying to find one tiny star in the billions and billions of stars in this galactic universe. Oh, one more thing. In many instances, the person who is asking the question...the questioner... doesn't really expect an answer, or more realistically, doesn't even *want* an answer."

"How did you get so smart, Beth?"

"Very good, Juanita. That is an excellent rhetorical question."

Juanita smiles, "*Bueno!*"

The referee blows his whistle. "Ok, teams—back on the field. Now let's play a good clean game. Don't start pushing and shoving or I'll call a foul on you and give the other team a free kick."

The Terminators get control of the ball and take it toward their goal. They are doing some fancy dribbling, trying to get the ball in a position for a good shot. Both teams are crowding around the Terminator goal trying to control the ball. Emily sees an opening to get to the ball. She moves closer to the crowd of players. She sees an opportunity to steal the ball. Suddenly Lucy (of the Terminators) pushes Emily from behind into a crowd of players who are fighting for the ball. Emily, trying to get her balance, accidentally knocks over several Terminator players and even a couple of her own Amigos.

The referee blows his whistle and flashes a yellow card and points to Emily. "Unnecessary roughness. Amigos! Free kick for the Terminators!"

Coach Brady of the Amigos jumps off the bench, starts to run onto the field and yells. "Come on Ref...Emily was pushed!"

"Get off the field! You know that's against the rules. I saw it all up close. Not 30 feet away like you."

"You'd have to be blind to make a call like that. That's totally an unfair call!"

"Sit back down on the bench, Coach!"

The Amigo coach is getting madder and madder. "I could have you banned as a referee for a call like that!"

All the Amigos run up to their Coach. "Take it easy, Coach. Settle down. Don't let them get 2 free kicks!"

The referee points to Coach Brady. "Sit down, Coach. I've got my hand on the red card! Sit down or I'll have you escorted off the field."

"Oh, yeah! By *whom*?"

"By that guard right over there." He points to a man in a uniform by the Amigo bench.

"Him? Ha! He's my younger brother. I've been kickin' his fanny all over a soccer field for over 20 years. He's not going to escort anybody anywhere!"

The referee is getting more aggravated by Coach Brady. "You better settle down Coach, or I will serve you with a Punitive Forfeiture."

"What the Sam Hill is that?"

"I can stop the game and award a victory to the Terminators

because of, #1 your attitude, #2 infringement of the rules of soccer, and #3, noncompliance of the orders of the referee. Are you going to sit down or not? I'm trying to be a nice guy and not give the Terminators two free kicks."

"Oh, yeah. You're a real nice guy all right." The coach sits down and puts his head in his hands.

"It's ok, Coach," says Emily. "This game isn't over. We'll get it back."

The referee holds the soccer ball as the Amigos make a line in front of the Terminator goal. #13 is preparing to kick.

Veronica turns to her teammates and gathers them around her. "Listen. I saw this in a game on TV once. It worked perfectly. We know #13 is a powerful kicker. I feel she's going for a high hard one."

Brenda Jean responds. "I think you're right Veronica. Don't you all?"

The rest of the team responds positively by nodding their heads, except for Emily and Ming.

"Actually, she *could* go high," says Emily.

"Or *low*," says Ming.

"But, if that's your feeling, Veronica," ...says Emily.

"You captain," ...praises Ming.

"Thanks for the vote of confidence, Emily and Ming." Emily turns her back and shakes her head knowing that Veronica, as usual, totally missed the point.

Veronica instructs the Amigo team, "So what we have to do is time a coordinated jump together, at the same time, synchronized, in unison. Got it?"

They all nod their heads, 'yes.' Veronica continues, "I'll watch #13 closely and then count her down— Three, two, one, jump! When I say, 'jump,' we all jump together! She'll never kick it over us...that's my feeling. Are you all with me?"

"We're with you, Veronica," her friends respond.

"I'm really excited, Veronica." says Brenda Jean. "But...ah..." squinching up her face, she continues, "I have to go to the bathroom."

"Just hold it, Brenda Jean," orders Veronica. "Get your priorities straight. We get a break after the kick."

"Ok...ok...ok," says Brenda Jean with a worried look. "But hurry!"

The referee blows his whistle. "Ready Terminators?"

"Yes!" Calls out #13.

"Ready Amigos?" asks the referee.

Veronica shouts, "Yes! Ref. We're more than ready!"

Brenda Jean yells out. "Yes...ready! ready! HURRY UP!"

Veronica gives Brenda a stern look. "Ok, go!"

The referee blows his whistle. With focused determination #13 approaches the soccer ball slowly. Then, with her head down and eyes on the ball she rushes toward the ball—she pulls back her right foot for the kick...but then...in total excitement, Brenda Jean yells out, "Three, two, one, jump!"

Veronica screams, "What? Wait! No! No! No!" Half of the Amigos jump, and the other half stand in confusion. With great accuracy and power #13 sends a low shot skimming across the grass. It passes directly underneath Veronica's feet into the net.

The referee blows his whistle, "Goal! Terminators 3, Amigos 2. Take a 10-minute break."

Brenda Jean runs for the bathroom. Veronica runs after her. "Come back here, Brenda Jean! Right now! Come back here, darn it!" Brenda Jean keeps running.

The Amigo coach buries his head in his hands. The Amigo fans look at each other in amazement. Emily and Ming give each other a big, sad hug.

The Terminators start cheering as they raise #13 on their shoulders and parade her around the field chanting. "Terminators! We will terminate you! Terminators! We will terminate you! Terminators! We will terminate you!"

In the bleachers, Diesel gets up and takes out some papers from a big envelop. He turns and addresses all the Amigo fans. "Listen Amigo fans. I think it's time we give some support to our team. Don't you?"

The Amigo fans respond. "Yes! Yes! Support our team! Support the Amigos!"

"Me and Grease wrote up some cheers. We'll pass them out and we can cheer together."

Diesel and Grease pass out the papers to all the Amigo fans. Then they go down in front of the bleachers and show them how it's done. "Ok, folks! Here goes! We'll keep saying it over and over, and when you get it, join in. Cheer real loud so our team can hear you!"

"The Amigos team is the world's best team! The Amigos Coach is the world's best Coach! The Amigo Fans are the world's best fans! We go where the Amigos go! Amigos play hard 'cause we root real hard! We love the Amigos when they win real big! We love the Amigos even if they don't win big! Yeah Amigos! Yeah Amigos!"

Ming takes Emily privately to the side and starts explaining things in detail to her as she raises one leg slightly and spins around and around. Emily watches Ming intensely and keeps nodding her head in agreement.

Since the Terminators made the last goal with a free kick by #13, the ball is placed in the middle of the field, and Ming waits for the referee to blow his whistle. When he does, she kicks the ball to Emily. They keep passing the ball back and forth between each other feinting off Terminators as they go. #13 goes to the goal to help the goalie prevent a goal by Ming or Emily. As Ming gets within a safe kicking distance from their goal, she calls out to Emily, "Swan Lake!" Emily starts to spin and spin in a pirouette. The spinning motion puts Emily's mind into a trance-like state where she believes she is not on a soccer field anymore but that she is the principle ballerina on a large stage performing Swan Lake for an audience in the bleachers. With each spin, she feels she is getting to the finale of the ballet. In perfect balance, Emily extends her right leg straight out and keeps spinning. With impeccable style and synchrony, Ming completes a flawless pass to Emily. Spinning and spinning, the music builds to a crescendo in Emily's head as she meets the ball with her extended right foot and sends it gently floating into the net like a white dove alighting in its nest.

The referee blows his whistle, "Terminators—3, Amigos—3!"

"My gosh," says Grease. "What was that? I never seen nuthin' like that before."

"That was a ballet spin you lunk head. Don't you know nothin' 'bout balletin?" scowls Diesel.

Diesel and Grease keep cheering Emily and Ming. "Way to go, Emily. Way to go, Ming. Keep it up. You'll beat those lunk heads yet."

Emily goes up to Ming and gives her a hug, "That was a perfect pass, Ming. You made it so easy for me. Thank you."

"Easy...you call that easy?" How many spins did you do?"

"I don't know?"

"You did more than a ballerina! Probably hundred!" says Ming.

"Oh, no...in the ballet Swan Lake the ballerina does 32."

"32?" says Ming, "You must did twice that!" Emily gives Ming another hug.

The referee blows his whistle. "Ten-minute warning till the end of the game." He puts the ball down at mid field. #9 of the Terminators kicks the ball to #13. #13 starts dribbling with determination toward her goal. She strikes the ball hard with a low solid kick that sends it with tremendous speed to a fellow Terminator, #8 waiting at her goal. #13 runs fast toward her goal being chased by the Amigos. #8 of the Terminators waits for #13 to approach her goal and then passes the ball to her. #13 looks around as she waits for the Amigos to catch up with her. The Amigos are running fast to try and stop #13 from making an easy goal. As #13 sees the Amigos approaching, she moves the ball slowly toward the goal. Delores, the Amigo goalie, remembering her last encounter with #13, crouches down to try and stop her legs from shaking and making ready for another powerful kick by #13. #13 moves the ball slowly toward Delores, but then she turns the ball back as if not interested in making a goal. Then four Amigos surround #13. With great skill #13 dribbles around and through her opponents, feinting left and right and doing a nutmeg through their legs at every opportunity. The Amigos are falling over their feet as they try to steal the ball from #13. Then, #13 starts using the referee as a shield. She dribbles behind the referee, and as the Amigos try to go around the referee to get to the ball, #13 puts her hands on the referee's hips and turns him to the left and then to the right and then spins him around as the Amigos lunge for the ball but are unable to capture it. Emily is standing back at mid field watching #13 make fools out of her team. She knows that at any time #13 could have easily made a goal, but her only desire was to make the Amigos look like silly clowns. Coach Bob of the Terminators is enjoying these antics so much he's laughing himself silly.

Having enough of #13's foolishness, Emily slowly approaches her near the Terminator goal. #13 sees Emily coming and starts to move the ball toward her, obviously trying to make a fool of her also. #13 does a few faints left and right as Emily just watches her antics. Then to prove her prowess #13 dribbles behind her back, trying to tease Emily to make a play for the ball, but Emily just stands back and watches her.

#13 then approaches Emily cautiously and does a rainbow kick over Emily's head. Emily, sensing the position of the ball in flight spins in a flash and quickly head butts the ball out of the reach of #13. #13, embarrassed at Emily's skill, runs after Emily and tries to do a leg sweep to catch the ball. Losing her balance from her leg sweep, #13 spreads her legs to secure her equilibrium. Seeing a perfect opportunity, Emily does a nutmeg between #13's outstretched feet and dribbles the ball far out of the reach of #13.

Instead of moving the ball toward her own goal, Emily starts pushing the soccer ball toward the Terminator goal. Both the Amigo team and Terminator team are shocked at what they're seeing. Voices can be heard from the bleachers, "What's Emily doing? Why is she going toward the Terminator goal?"

Diesel and Grease can be heard over the rest of the crowd, "Emily, you're going the wrong way! Turn around! Turn around!"

The coaches, the fans, even Fritz and Pegasus seem to ask, "What is Emily doing?"

Emily takes the ball about 20 feet from the Terminator goal. The Terminator goalie looks confused. Then in utter shock, everyone sees Emily tap the top of the ball with her foot bouncing it up to her knee. From there Emily again taps the soccer ball with her knee to head height. As the ball descends to a perfect height Emily leans to her left and slams the ball high and hard over the goalie's head—into the Terminator's net.

A resounding shock of disbelief by the crowd can be felt all over the field. Every person in the crowd, except for Dr. Yang, looks to their neighbor and starts asking questions, 'What is she doing? What was she thinking? Is she mentally confused because of the stress of the game?'

Dr. Yang with a slightly 'knowing' smile on his lips, closes his eyes and bows undetected in Emily's direction.

Laughing hard, the referee takes several tries before he can blow his whistle. Finally, he can blow his whistle, "Goal for the Terminators: Score—Terminators 4, Amigos 3".

The Terminator team and their Coach are laughing and shouting out loud, "Gracias Amigos! Gracias!"

Emily goes to her bench. Frantically, her Coach runs up to her. "What did you do, Emily? What did you do?"

"I stopped #13 from making fools of my Amigos, that's what I did Coach! *Nobody* makes fun of my team."

"What do you think we're going to do now, Emily?" Coach Brady asks.

"We're going to win this game, Coach. That's what we're going to do. *Just watch!*"

Meanwhile, Dr. Yang sees how distressed Bibou is. "Bibou... may I call you you, Bibou?"

"At this point you can call me anything...I mean...what did she do? I don't think I can..."

"Good, I don't want you to think. Let's go down to the field. I want to talk to you."

Dr. Yang and Bibou climb down from the bleachers. Dr. Yang motions to Bibou to follow him behind the bleachers. Bibou kicks the dirt, "How could she do such a thing? She's blown it. All she ever talks about is winning, and now she's thrown this game away. I can't believe it."

Dr. Yang consoles Bibou. "You are too close to her, Bibou. You don't see past the little girl. She is maturing beautifully. It took incredible courage, self-confidence, and psychological intelligence to do what she did. She blew everybody's mind. Especially the other team and their coach. Now they don't know what to expect. What do you expect from a girl who will sacrifice a game to stand up for what she believes is morally right? 'No one is going to treat my team that way,' is basically what she said by doing that."

Bibou asks, "What about winning the game?"

"She has gone beyond winning—from *winning* to *honor*, to *courage*. Her courage has totally confused the Terminators and their coach. What kind of person would do this—a frightened person, a weak person, a person who has given up? I don't think so, and I believe the Terminators are going to find out very soon what kind of person Emily really is."

Dr. Yang points to the Terminator Coach. "Bibou, I want you to look at the Terminator Coach. Before, he was laughing and chanting, 'Gracias Amigos' with the rest of the team; but look at him now. You see what he's doing? He's pulling the hair on the side of his head, why? Because he's trying to calm down the amygdala part of his brain. The amygdala deals with fear, anger, frustration, and threatening situations. That's what he's dealing with now. That's what Emily has done to him...she's put his brain into a tailspin... like a plane ready to crash. Now look...see what he's doing now... he's pounding his forehead with his fist. That's because that's the part of the brain that deals with problem solving or how to adequately interpret risk and danger. Emily has created a situation in his brain where he doesn't know what to do next.

"Whoever they thought Emily was... they now know that isn't her. She has them totally confused. They now fear her more than ever because they don't understand her—which is a more powerful weapon—more powerful than those points she gave them. She has raised herself to a level of competitiveness that no one on that field has ever seen before or may never see again, and they totally don't understand it. It's even so new that Emily probably doesn't understand it herself. She was in the moment. She just reacted from the heart. Nothing is more beautiful than that. This feeling within her is as real and as true as the hair on her head."

Dr. Yang, continues, "Now #13 realizes she is playing against an opponent she has never faced before. A player that thinks beyond the game—a player that not only can skillfully control the soccer ball, the dribbling and the shooting but a player with great finesse and adroit skills who has entered the mind of her adversaries and is manipulating their psychology and mental constructs with great ingenuity.

"Bibou, you, your wife and her parents have raised a remarkable young woman who is shoulders above the 'norm.' In my practice as an acupuncturist I deal with a lot of people with intense personal challenges. Emily is strong and capable and will achieve wonderful things in her life...for herself and maybe more importantly, for others.

"In Chinese the word for this kind of courage is—*Yongqi.*"

Dr. Yang takes a stick and scratches the Chinese characters for *Yongqi* in the dirt. "Take a picture of that, date it, frame it and remember this day forever. It is a milestone."

At the Amigo bench, Emily puts her arm on Veronica's shoulder and guides her off to a spot away from the others. "Veronica, you know where we are now?"

"Uh...Cincinnati?"

"Yes...but...more importantly, we're at the 'moment of truth.'"

"I've heard of that. What does it mean exactly?"

"Veronica, it is a moment when we are being tested. A decision has to be made—a crisis has to be faced. Are you up for that challenge?"

"I uh...can you say those things again?"

"It means we have to 'cowboy up,' you've heard of that right? You're from California."

"Yeah...that means we have to be tough...like cowboys!"

"Yeah, or cowgirls. Right?"

"Right!"

"You're the captain of this team!"

"You're right. I know that," agrees Veronica.

"Ok, good Veronica. Because, *you're* going to blow the minds of the Terminators with my grandfather Bibou's Criss-Cross-Conundrum!"

"Me? You mean you're going to let me try and kick the goal on the Criss-Cross Thingy?"

"Not try, Veronica. You're going to make that goal. Just remember, Veronica you're the Captain of the team. You're going to pull us out this hole. Right?"

Veronica shouts, "Right!"

Emily bends down and rubs the instep area of Veronica's right shoe. "This spot, Veronica. Not the toe. Not the toe. Please, not the toe. This is the spot for accuracy and power. Got it?"

"Got it! Not the toe."

"Coach," calls Emily. "We've got a special belated birthday present for you. We were working on it when you were at your birthday party. I hope you like it", Then, under her breath, "And I hope we get it right."

"Oh, I'm sure I'll like it. What is it? I hope it's the soccer trophy."

"So do we, Coach. Cross your fingers. Rather... Criss-Cross your fingers."

Coach Brady gathers his team around him. "Listen, Amigos. We're in a tight spot. But you've been playing a great game. Things will change. Defense! Defense! Defense! You'll catch 'em. Don't be afraid. Take those shots."

Dr. Yang is sitting in the bleachers next to Bibou, Grandmother Kay-Kay and Emily's mom and dad, Sarah and Steve. Emily gets Bibou's attention and crosses her forearms signaling him that they are going to do the Criss-Cross-Conudrum. Bibou shakes his head, "No, no," and then puts his face in his hands and seems to start praying.

The referee blows his whistle. "Ok teams you've got 2 minutes then back on the field."

Veronica touches Emily on the arm. "Thanks, Emily, for having faith in me. Listen, I know that sometimes I could act more polite and stuff like that... I get confused. It's really tough being rich... *and* pretty."

"Why?"

"Because everybody expects so much from you, and everybody wants to be your friend, and...sometimes I wonder if maybe I should..."

"Focus! Veronica...focus!" scolds Emily.

"Yes...you're right...focus. Gosh, Emily you're so levelheaded. I wish I was more like you sometime. How does my hair look?"

"Marvelous, Veronica...pulchritudinous!"

"Pool-chi-what? Now I know that's a bad word!"

"It means beautiful, Veronica...statuesque."

"Where did you learn such a big word?"

"From Bibou...by grandfather. He's really smart. He was a Montessori teacher."

"Monty who?" Vernonica asks.

"Veronica...Concentrate...please," begs Emily. "Ok, Amigos let's go! It's time to blow some minds with the Criss-Cross-Conundrum."

Amigos in unison: "Right on!"

The referee blows his whistle. "Ok, 2 minutes then back on the field."

Emily tells the team, "We're going to do the Criss-Cross-Co-nundrum now, and Veronica's going to kick the goal. I'm going to get the fans involved. You all say a little prayer...or maybe a big prayer." Emily goes to the Amigo fans in the bleachers. "Listen Fans you want the Amigos to win, right?"

"Right!" they all respond.

"Ok, here's what you have to do to help us. It's really easy. You just do this rhythmic chant while you clap your hands: Boom, boom, clap; boom, boom, clap. Let me hear you do it!"

The Amigo fans chant, "Boom, boom, clap. Boom, boom, clap."

"Very good," says Emily. "Now you stomp your feet in the

bleachers for the 'boom, boom'. Try that!"

The crowd does that, and it rocks the bleachers.

"One last thing, fans," says Emily. "When you stomp your feet you sing really loud, "We will, we will sock Sock you! Clap!" Get it? It's sock you! Like soccer. It's very important. Thanks! Watch for my signal!!!"

The crowd cheers Emily as she runs out on to the field. "Go get'em Emily!"

The game starts. Since the last goal was made at the Terminator's goal, the Amigos get the ball at center field. Brenda Jean passes the ball to Veronica. Veronica goes down field to her goal. She sees that Ming is open. She tries to pass to Ming but kicks the ball too hard, and it is intercepted by #9 of the Terminators. #9 watches the position of #13 and starts quickly toward her goal. Emily sees another Terminator going to fill the space 20 feet in front their goal. Emily waits like a leopard ready to pounce. #9 passes the ball to another Terminator. Emily anticipating that pass, steals the ball. Quickly and skillfully she dribbles toward her end of the field. When she gets to the halfway mark, she stops by putting her foot on top of the ball. She looks at the Amigo fans in the bleachers and calls to them, "Boom, Boom, Clap! Boom Clap!"

The crowd responds with the chant, and soon the bleachers are rocking with the rhythm, Boom, Boom, Clap! Boom, Boom, Clap! The other Amigos form a line 15 feet in front of their goal. The Terminators and their coach hear this mysterious chanting and don't know what to think. Veronica situates herself behind her teammates that have formed the line. Emily waves to the Amigo fans to continue the chanting:

"We will, we will sock you! Clap! Sock you, clap! We will, we will, sock you! Clap, sock you! Clap!" They keep up the chant as play continues.

The bleachers are roaring with the chant. Emily moves the ball behind the line where Veronica is standing. She nods to Veronica. Veronica nods back and brushes her hair back.

With intense fierceness #13 is watching Emily who is taking the ball toward Veronica. With great agility, #13 jumps between her own players and steals the ball from Emily. #13 takes the ball to the corner to get away from Emily. Emily is hot on her trail. #13 turns around and volleys the ball back and forth between her feet. Emily thinks, 'I know what she's going to do—a feint.'

It's exactly what #13 does. Emily has observed that #13 is left-footed. So, #13 feints to the right and then slides the ball to the left. As she does, Emily jumps to #13's left side and steals the ball.

Emily heads for Veronica. #13 sees what Emily is doing so she also heads for Veronica to stop Emily from giving the ball to Veronica. Veronica is getting more nervous as the tension builds.

The Amigo fans keep chanting, "We will, we will sock you! Clap! Sock you! Clap! WE will, we will sock you! Clap!"

Everyone is chanting loudly except Dr. Yang who is sitting quietly with his eyes closed.

Emily has her back to the goal as she tries to get the ball in position for Veronica to kick the goal. Suddenly #13 appears out of nowhere and chases Emily into the corner of the field. #13 is getting ready to make a steal. Emily's mind is panicking. "She's got me cornered. How do I get the ball to Veronica in time?" Seconds seem like hours. Suddenly Emily hears a familiar voice bellow out from the crowd, "Rainbow Emily, rainbow!" It's Diesel. The sound of Diesel's voice shatters #13's concentration. In that split second of Diesel's command, time stands still for both #13 and Emily. #13 loses her concentration. Emily sees #13's head turn toward Diesel. Emily knows what she has to do—the 'Rainbow Kick' that she's practiced a million times in her head.

In a flash, Emily lifts the ball with her right foot to the back of the left leg. The ball slides down to her left heel. Leaning forward Emily kicks the ball with her heel over both her head and over #13's head. Quickly Emily gets to the ball leaving #13 alone, scratching her head.

Emily stops the ball with her right foot right in front of

Veronica. Emily sees the Terminators ready to charge the ball. She calls out, "Amigos," and raises both arms above her head. Then she shouts, "Down Amigo!" Then Emily and all the Amigos rake their arms down with great force sending the Terminators into a daze.

Then Emily shouts, "Dive!"

The Amigos then dive to the ground and lie flat opening a big space for Veronica to kick the ball. Veronica is ready. She takes two big steps and connects the soccer ball perfectly with the instep of her right shoe.

The ball soars strong and hard and is going toward the left pole of the goal. 'It's not going to make it. It's not going to make it into the net,' people shout. Then suddenly, with a great spin the ball curves inward out of the reach of the goalie.

"She did it! The Fans cheer, "Goal for the Amigos. Score tied."

"Goal!" Shouts the referee. "Amigo's—4, Terminator's—4!!!"

Emily looks into the bleachers and spots Bibou. She sends him a 'thumbs up.' He immediately stands up and with great gusto, returns a double 'thumbs up!'

The Amigos jump around Veronica chanting her name: "Veronica! Veronica! Veronica! You did it! You did it!"

"I know! I know! I think it even curved a little bit. Did everyone see that?"

"Oh, yeah, Veronica! I think you're right! It curved right into the net!"

"Veronica you kicked a banana!" cheers Emily.

"I did? I didn't see any bananas."

"No," explains Emily. "When you make a ball curve like that, they call it a 'Banana Kick.'"

"Oh, my," exclaims Veronica, "A banana how exciting!" She then waves to her father in the stands as she sees other parents patting him on the back.

"Oh, gosh, I'm serious! Serious! Serious! I *really* need a coke!" gasps Veronica, wiping her mouth with the back of her hand.

Emily gets in Veronica's face. "Veronica! Focus! No cokes! No cokes! We've got a game to win! I'll buy you a case of cokes after the game!"

"Really?!!" Exclaims Veronica. "No, not really Veronica..." Says Emily, rolling her eyes.

The referee blows his whistle, "This is the 2-minute warning. Only 2 more minutes to play. Terminator's ball."

At the Amigo bench all the players have gathered around Coach Brady. "There's only time for one more goal shot in this game. The Terminators have got the ball. What do we have to do?"

"We have to get that ball!" exclaims Emily.

"That's right! Get that ball! And then what?"

"Set up a shot." says Ming.

"Very good, you're all thinking. Now you can do this thing. Don't panic. Two minutes is a long time."

"Unless we don't have the ball..." says Emily.

"Right Emily! So, let's get that ball. But no fouling. Please!"

The referee blows his whistle. "Let's go Amigos! Don't make me call you for a delay of game!"

"Oh, brother..." says Coach Brady shaking his head. "Ok, Amigos. This is your game. You've beaten them already. Just finish them off."

Emily stops two of her teammates as they approach the field. "Listen Becky and Toni. When #13 gets the ball and there is a distance between her and #9, I want you to rush her with your arms flailing and screaming as loud as you can. Make her panic for just a second that's all you have to do. Can you do that?"

"It's done, Emily. Count on it," say Becky and Toni. Then they enthusiastically run out onto the field. As Emily walks out to the field, she sees a cat hypnotized by a bird in a tree. The cat is motionless. Her breathing indiscernible. The bird is in her own world looking at an insect. The cat is in his world waiting for the exact moment.

The referee places the ball down in the middle of the field and blows his whistle.

Emily shakes the thoughts from her mind and comes back to her soccer game. #9 kicks the ball to #13. They both methodically dribble the ball down toward their goal. Emily, staying in the middle of the field, makes her way down toward the Terminator's goal. She sees #13 making room between her and #9.

Emily whispers to herself, "Ok, Becky and Toni get ready...get ready...now!"

As if Becky and Toni could telepathically read Emily's thoughts, they raise their arms and screaming charge #13. Slightly concerned, #13 looks for #9. #13 thinks, '*She's too far away.*'

Emily feels the moment. The cat and bird flash in her mind. #13 shoots a low pass toward #9. She leaps. "I've got it! I've got it!" She steals the ball and starts 118 down the field toward her goal. The crowd is standing—cheering Emily on.

#13 seems to bound like a panther as she springs down the field to catch Emily. Emily can feel her coming with her great speed. She momentarily turns to see where #13 is and loses control of the ball. In a split second #13 steals the ball back.

In shock, Emily is after her. She thinks, '*I've got to force her into a corner.*' Emily starts to crowd her. She knows that #13 can get around her if she has a chance. '*I've got to keep crowding her but not too close*'.

Emily crowds #13 into the corner. Then Emily rushes her. Under pressure #13 makes a mistake. She turns her back to Emily. She can't see Emily. Emily bends over keeping her position close to the ground.

Then Emily spreads her legs wide apart and thinks, '*Take the bait, 13, take the bait*'.

#13 turns, takes a quick glance of Emily with her legs spread. She takes the bait and shoots a nutmeg between Emily's legs. Instantly Emily spins, and she has the ball. She is near her goal. Emily can feel all the Terminators are coming in for an attack. She moves the ball to the sideline.

From the Terminator's bench Juanita can be heard shouting loudly, "Mono e mono."

Beth asks her, "What does that mean, Juanita?"

"It really means, 'Hand-to-hand,' but the Gringos thinks it means, 'Man-to-man.' We think that's really funny, but we don't correct them. Gringos don't like to be corrected by Hispanics. So, we shut up to keep the peace. Don't tell anybody but I hope Emily keeps the ball and makes goal."

"I do too," says Beth.

Juanita says, "Bueno!"

#13 tries desperately to steal the ball. But Emily protects the ball with great finesse. Then Emily stops the ball by putting her foot on top of it. A victor has captured her prey.

Emily rolls the ball back making more room between her and #13. She seems to be teasing #13 to try for a steal. #13 doesn't move. Then Emily pulls the ball back a few more inches. They look at each other like animals poised for an attack. Emily is thinking about the Acupuncture point 'Stomach 36' just below the knee, that Dr. Yang had told her about. '*It is the most powerful point of the body*'; she remembers him saying. '*If you treat it clockwise it will give you energy. If you treat it counterclockwise it will weaken you*'.

Then, as if unable to control her instincts, #13 jumps for the ball. As she does, Emily makes a powerful kick touching the ball on the outside creating a counterclockwise spin. It hits #13 on the leg at 'Stomach 36' and sends her to the ground as the ball rolls out of bounds.

The referee blows his whistle and says, "Amigo's ball. It touched #13 before it went out of bounds. My time out!"

#13 is limping around in circles. "Oh, my knee. I can't feel my knee. It's numb. I've gotta sit down."

Emily goes up to #13. "Don't worry. It's only temporary. You'll be ok in a few minutes."

By then Coach Bob has run over from the Terminator bench and is kneeling next to his star player. "Are you ok? Can you play? There's only 30 seconds left."

"I think I can play, Coach. Just give me a minute." The referee hands the ball to Ming. "Thank you, sir," smiles Ming. Ming moves close to Emily and whispers something quickly into her ear. Emily takes a place near the Amigo goal and starts rubbing the acupuncture points on top of her head, beneath her kneecap and then she puts both thumbs behind her back and presses beneath her rib cage. Then she signals Ming with two thumbs up.

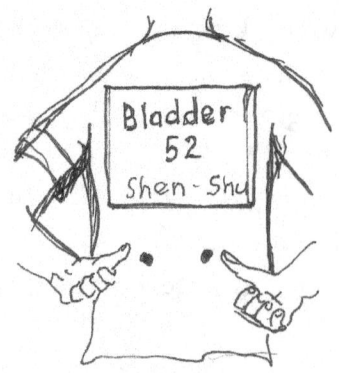

Ming takes the soccer ball and walks about 10 feet behind the boundary line. Diesel and Grease are getting very excited and worried. "Grease do you see what I'm seeing?"

Grease puts his hands on his head. "I hope I'm not, but I think I am."

Diesel turns back to Dr. Yang and he yells out. "Is she going to do a flip throw

Dr. Yang cups his hands around his mouth and yells down to Grease and Diesel. "It looks like it!"

Grease asks, "Has she done a flip throw before?"

Dr. Yang returns. "I think she mentioned it...once...If I remember correctly."

Grease and Diesel fold their hands in prayer and look to the sky.

Bibou asks, Dr. Yang. "Did he say, 'flip throw?' That sounds dangerous."

Dr. Yang explains. "It entails doing a front handspring with the ball in your hands. She will take about 5 steps, plant the ball on the ground and then fling her body over the ball, landing on her two feet just behind the out of bounds line. Then, using her core muscles, she forces her torso up straight again. Using this momentum, she flings the ball in one violent motion toward the goal—like a giant sling shot!"

Bibou rubs his head. "It, sounds exciting, complicated and dangerous."

Dr. Yang smiles, "Ming is very courageous. A good athlete loves danger."

Bibou asks, "Can you make a goal from a flip throw?"

"If you could, I think she'd try, but it doesn't count," Says Dr. Yang. "When performed correctly, it can place the ball perfectly within striking range of the goal."

The Amigo fans are again on the edge of their seats. All the players of the Amigos and Terminators are assembled near the

Amigo goal. #13 can be seen favoring her sore leg. Everyone watches as Ming goes back about 10 feet from the out-of-bounds line. She holds the ball in both her hands and raises it a few times above her head. Ball in hand, she prepares to get a running start. Ming nods to Emily. Emily nods back and then starts to rub the three points Dr. Yang instructed her when he treated her with acupuncture at his home: St-36 below her knees, Kd-23 behind her back, and Du-20 on top of her head.

Ming looks over to her bench as Coach Brady holds his head and turns his back to the field. "I can't watch. I can't watch."

Emily makes a fist and swings it over her head. Ming smiles and bows to Emily. Ming looks back at Coach Brady.

Coach Brady swings back around to the soccer field. "I've got to watch. I've got to watch." He calls out to Ming. "Give it all you've got, Ming. You can do it!"

Surprisingly, it gets very silent on the soccer field and in the bleachers.

The referee calls out. "21 seconds to go." Then, he blows his whistle.

Ming lowers her head. She thinks, *Five steps. Five steps.* She starts. She builds momentum as she goes. *Five, four, three, two...* she plants the ball on the ground. She flings her body over the ball and then in one violent motion her acrobatic flip launches the ball like a rocket 20 yards far and high toward the Amigo goal. Ming lands on both feet and freezes to a standing point just behind the out-of-bounds line.

There is no breeze. The wind waits within the trees. The crowd hasn't taken a breath in the last two minutes. Players from both teams watch the ball as it hovers high above their heads like a large bird with invisible wings looking for a place to land.

Then the ball, as if seeing Emily back behind the crowd of players, pauses for a second and then begins to drop. For Emily, the ball descends in silent slow motion. She moves back a few steps, watches the ball carefully and then approaches a spot where she knows she will converge with the ball at the exact place to make the most effective and perfectly timed impact. Emily is ready. As the ball sails toward the goal, the crowd starts a countdown as the digital clock on the score board moves to the end of the game.

The crowd counts loudly, "Eight, Seven...(the ball is fall- ing)..."Six, Five..." Emily standing with her back to the goal, prepares herself.

Crowd, "Four...Three..."

Emily takes two large strides. Then as if she is on her trampoline, she feels her body lift—her feet moving with grace and dexterity above her head. She sees the ball. The moment has arrived. With great confidence, precision and power Emily's right leg extends, and the strings of her right shoe connect with the soccer ball, slamming it with tremendous power and speed over the head of the Terminator goalie, almost burning a hole in the Amigo net.

The referee blows his whistle, "Goal! Game! Amigos—5, Terminators—4. Amigos are the champions!"

A thrilling wave of '*Victory!*' reverberates throughout the whole soccer assembly.

Diesel's voice can be heard over all the fans. "Yes! Yes! Yes! A perfect bicycle! Emily did a perfect bicycle! We won! We won!"

The Amigo fans almost fly out of the bleachers. Totally thrilled and out of control, they run onto the field, hugging, spinning, dancing and rolling on the grass. People who would rarely think of a close encounter with certain Amigo fans are found hugging and squeezing everyone in sight...even Diesel and Grease.

As the Amigo players are piling on each other, Fritz runs out on the field, and it looks like he's trying to do a flip himself.

The crowd is going wild with tears of joy as they dance and sing and keep cheering, "Amigos! Amigos! Gracias! Gracias!"

Diesel whispers to Grease, "Hey man, are you thinkin' what I'm thinkin'?"

Grease smiles, "Well, I hope I'm thinkin' what you're thinkin'! But if I'm not thinkin' what you're thinkin', then maybe somebody else is thinkin' what you're thinking, and if that's happin', then that's *really* not good so we better hurry up and go find Emily and Ming really fast...is what I'm thinkin'!"

"Ok, let's go!" says Diesel. They take off running toward the Amigo bench. The Amigos are going over to the Terminator's bench to congratulate them. But Emily and Ming are waiting behind as they see Bibou and Dr. Yang coming in their direction.

Diesel stops Grease. "Let's just wait here while they talk to their family and friends. Then we'll talk to Emily and Ming when they're alone. Because first we gotta practice how we're gonna ask'em."

"Good idea," says Grease. "But first we gotta make sure we're gonna ask them a question we think we've been talkin' about, but are not really sure yet. Does that make sense? I'm getting' a little confused."

"No, that's good thinkin' Grease. I think all this excitement has made you a little smarter."

"Yeah, my brain feels like it's buzzin'!"

The Terminator Coach has been staring in utter silence at Emily and the Amigo bench as they are celebrating their victory. Then with an intense feeling of determination, he walks slowly across the soccer field in the direction of the Amigo bench.

Ming taps Emily on the shoulder. "Emily, don't look now, but guess who's coming over to our side of field." Emily starts to turn around. Ming stops her. "No, don't look, get ready for big surprise."

"Oh, boy! Is it going to be fun?"

"I don't know if *fun* is right word," says Ming. Unable to resist, Emily turns around and sees the Terminator Coach closing in on the Amigo bench. Bibou and Dr. Yang also see the Terminator Coach. Bibou address Dr. Yang. "Dr. Yang am I seeing things, or is smoke coming out of that Coaches ears?"

"I think you're seeing things, Bibou...I hope," says Dr. Yang.

They both move closer to the action, in case Emily and Ming need some support. As they get closer, Bibou and Dr. Yang see the Terminator Coach hold his hand out to Emily. Emily responds by holding out her hand to him. They shake hands.

"Hello, Emily. My name is Bob. I'm the Terminator Coach."

"Oh, I was wondering what you were doing over there today." She and Ming chuckle. "Just kidding, sir! Very happy to meet you."

"So, you've got a good sense of humor too. You're quite the talented young lady."

"Thank you. I'd like you to meet my good friend, Ming."

"You also played a fine game, Ming. That was a beautiful butterfly kick you laid on us."

"Thank you, Bob," smiles Ming.

Bob addresses Emily in a serious tone, "Emily, I want to let you know something. In all the years I've been coaching, we haven't won every game we've played...in case you were wondering." He chuckles along with Emily and Ming. "In all the defeats we have encountered, I have never come over to congratulate the team that beat us. I usually just gather my team together and make it very clear to them why, in so many maybe unkind, unrepeatable words, why we were crushed by a lesser component. But today I'm breaking my stubborn streak. I didn't say an unkind word to my team. Because, you didn't just beat my team. You beat me! And the horrible thing about it is...I don't know how you did it. I wanted to let you know I painfully enjoyed watching you take us to the cleaners. But the interesting thing is that you did *more* than beat us. You taught us a lesson –a lesson in soccer. The thing is, I can't figure out what the lesson was. That's why I came over here to ask you. What did you do? I keep wracking my brain! What did you teach us?"

Emily stands speechless...for a few seconds. "Coach, I taught you two things. You're smart so let's see if you can figure them out. Here's the question. What are the two best weapons against a good team in soccer?"

"Well what I'd probably say, after 15 years of coaching, is talent and intense passion," he says, feeling proud of his answer.

Emily helps him out. "Those are very good weapons, but let me ask it this way, Coach. What went through your mind when I kicked that goal for your Terminators?"

"Surprise, shock, disbelief! I really wasn't happy about it because it was so strange, I couldn't figure it out. I couldn't believe it! It blew my mind! I guess that covers it."

"That's right, Coach. Surprise! Shock! That's the first weapon. "Now, what is the second weapon?"

The Coach scratches his head and then, in an embarrassed tone he says, "Well, let me think." He looks up to the clouds and then to some birds flying overhead. "I'm exhausted from that game and keep seeing you kicking that goal for us over and over again in my head and can't figure out why. My mind's a blank. I was totally confused then, and I'm still totally confused now. That's why I came over here to try and get some answers."

Excited, Emily shakes the Coach's hand. "Congratulations, Coach! You got it! You figured out the two best weapons in a soccer match...according to Emily Hall – surprise and confusion! *Surprise* them with something unbelievable, and they get so totally *confused* they can't think straight, and then you are totally in control of the game. They just might as well go sit on their bench and watch you kick as many goals as you want. *Surprise* and *confusion*, who'd a thunk?"

Coach Bob smiles at her. "Emily, I think you're going to be a great soccer player someday, and maybe in time, even a great coach. I'm so impressed that you can come up with these profound concepts at such an early age."

"You know, Coach. I didn't come up with them. They came up by themselves and from the input from all my friends like Ming, her dad and my family. You know, practice, playing and learning from people you love, is like planting many different seeds in a field. You don't really know what you've planted but all of a sudden delicious and nutritious surprises spring up and start to grow..."

Ming jumps in, "And maybe even some beautiful flowers." All three laugh together.

Coach Bob shakes Emily's hand. "I can't wait till our next encounter, Emily. I'll be ready for anything, and I'm sure you'll have many new surprises for me. Great meeting you, and you too Ming."

"Thank you, Coach," say Emily and Ming.

"Take care, Coach Bob." says Ming. "You know there is international formula in Chinese and every language for winning every event you encounter. *Ai zhengfule suoyou ren,* 'love conquers all.'"

"I'll try to keep than in my mind, Ming. Thank you."

"I'm going to run and get a treat. I'm starving." says Ming. "I'll be back, Emily."

Ming leaves as #13 comes up and Coach Bob starts to leave. #13 says to Coach Bob, "I'll see you at the bus in a few minutes, Coach."

"Take your time," he replies.

Emily goes up to #13 shakes her hand and gives her a big hug. "Hi, I'm Emily."

#13 smiles. "Oh yeah, I'm very aware of that!" They both laugh.

"How's your leg?" asks Emily.

"Good as new...somehow it feels even better. I can't figure that out."

"I'll tell you about that later," says Emily. She sees Ming approaching, and she motions for her to come over. "I'd like you to meet my friend Ming."

Stephanie says, "Great game, Ming."

Ming mimics like she is afraid. "Oh, my it...#13—terror of Terminators." Then she laughs and holds out her hand.

#13 holds out her hand. "Hi, I'm Stephanie." They shake hands. "That was a beautiful 'butterfly kick' you performed out there today, Ming. I might have been hallucinating, but just before you made that great kick, I thought I saw a butterfly flying around your head."

"Oh yeah, that my pet, 'Buttercup.' She follow me everywhere I go." Ming winks to Emily who is smiling and shaking her head. "Just kidding. Chinese humor. Nice to meet you, Stephanie. Emily, I'm going to find my dad and see if I can squeeze a little more allowance out of him after making that butterfly kick. It looks like you both have lot to discuss. It was a great experience playing with you today, Stephanie. Thank you. *Xie xie.*"

"And thank you, Ming, *xie xie*...I guess that means *thank you.*"

Stephanie waves goodbye to Ming. "You got it!" Ming waves to her as she heads for the bleachers.

Emily looks Stephanie straight in the eyes. "You are really a great player, Stephanie. You pulled the best out of us today. You made us play like we've never played before. I could never have done what I did in this game if it wasn't for your skills and determination that brought out maneuvers in me that I didn't even know were there. I want to thank you for that, and I feel that we really didn't win over you, but that we shared in a beautiful experience. The game could easily have gone either way."

Then Stephanie gives Emily a big hug. "You are a wonderful player also. I really enjoyed not only playing with you but also watching the way you maneuver with the ball. You look like you're dancing with the ball. I think I'm going to start practicing that. It would be fun. But the most important thing I think we learned from your team is camaraderie—we have never played a team that had so much love and friendship for each other. I really appreciate the way you worked with the other girls in letting them take chances to make a goal. Thank you."

Then Emily turns to the crowd, takes Stephanie's hand and holds it up high saying, "We, the Amigos, and all our fans, want to congratulate the Terminators on an incredible game. And, we want to invite them back here to play again. Who knows, maybe one day we'll be playing together on the same team. That would be incredible! Hip Hip Hooray for the Terminators!"

The crowd joins in, "Hip Hip Hooray for the Terminators."

Stephanie takes Emily aside. "Emily, thank you for that nice gesture, but what I really want to do is...apologize for my antics today. I know I stepped over the bounds with all that 'Gracias Amigos and Adios Amigos.' I should have been more polite and had better sportsmanship or sports-woman-ship out there."

"You know I think your coach has a lot to do with that. He's pretty tough on your team, isn't he?"

"Yes, he is."

"And I bet he pushes and drives you girls really hard. I also bet that the way you acted was because that is the way *he* would play the game...with a lot of antagonism. We don't believe in that. We believe in hard work."

"You're very perceptive Emily. And you're very right about our coach. I've played a lot of soccer games in my short life—I love soccer—I practice every day for hours. I hope to keep playing for many years, and, maybe, if I'm lucky, I might become a professional. But I'll tell you one thing—that game today will stick in my mind and heart forever. I want to thank you for that experience, Emily. I'm very lucky to have met a person that I would hope to become more like some day."

Emily says, "Thank you. But the only reason we played tough today is because you brought it out in us. I never would have done the things I did today...I wouldn't have even thought I could do them. But it was you that gave us a tremendous challenge because of your incredible abilities. You made us rise to heights we couldn't even have imagined before today's game. Thank you so much for that."

"If I did that, it was worth losing the game."

"You didn't lose the game. That scoreboard doesn't tell the

whole story. What really happened out there was not measured in numbers. It was measured in what we learned from each other in ways that maybe we can't even understand today—but if we keep this game in our hearts, someday it will become clear, and it will come to mean a great many things to us."

They hug each other.

"Stephanie, I want to ask you about something," asks Emily. "How does your team deal with your coach and the way he wants you to play the game?"

"Yes, he's tough. A lot of girls can't take it, and they quit with tears in their eyes. But he's had a lot of unfortunate things happen in his life and in his family. Soccer helps him forget all those things for a while. So, his anger and temperament aren't toward us. It's a way he expresses the grief he's going through. We understand... so we don't desert him. We try and support him in any way we can."

Emily asks, "I don't want to pry but...do you mind if I ask? What causes him so much stress?"

"Well, he was a really good soccer player. The pros were after him, and then Vietnam happened, and he had to go. After that... well he was older, and he had changed a lot. Then his son started to shine as a soccer player. It made Coach Bob really proud and really happy. Like his dad, teams were after him. The University of Cincinnati wanted to give him a full scholarship. The family was so happy for both Coach Bob and his son. Then, during one game there was a big pile up and unfortunately his leg got broken." A tear starts to form in Stephanie's eye.

"It's ok, you don't have to go on..." says Emily.

"I'm sorry...sometimes I get too emotional about this whole thing."

"No worries," Emily comforts her.

"So, what happened was...when my brother broke his..." Stephanie stops short.

Emily with eyes wide open. "Whoa! Wait a minute! Did you say...*brother*?"

Stephanie nods her head, "Yes. I'm sorry I shouldn't have gotten so..."

"No, no... that's ok. You mean...if he's your brother and he's the son of Coach Bob...then I guess...you're the daughter of Coach Bob. Holy moly...Right? Now this whole drama makes more sense."

"Please don't tell anyone. I promised my dad..."

"Don't worry I won't tell anyone."

Ming returns and sees that something has been going on. "Everybody ok here?"

"Everything's fine, Ming. We were talking about Stephanie's brother who is a really good soccer player..."

"Well, if he half as good as Stephanie he more than 'really good.'"

Emily continues, "Anyhow, he hurt his leg really badly. Actually, he broke it in a soccer match. He had a scholarship to UC but then he lost it."

"I see where this going." says Ming and continues, "Stephanie, my father is acupuncturist and I broke my leg also. The medical doctors want to remove it, but my father say, 'No,' and he start working on it, and I still have leg today."

Stephanie says, "He must have done a really good job the way you were playing today."

"Yeah, I guess so. Why don't you come with me, and we talk to my dad?"

Emily says, "Ming, I'm going to see if Coach Bob wants to get in on this conversation. He's very good friends with Stephanie's brother. You guys start over and I'll get Coach Bob."

"*Mei Wenti*, Emily. Come on Stephanie. Follow me."

"Thanks a lot. You Amigos certainly are friendly," says Stephanie.

"That why they call us Amigos," smiles Ming.

"Ming, was that a Chinese word you just spoke?" asks Stephanie. "No, it French..." Ming laughs. "Sorry, Chinese humor. Can't help it. Come on I teach you a few words on way over...just nice sweet words. Americans always want to know naughty words. Why that?" They both laugh as they start walking toward the bleachers.

At that moment Emily's grandmother, Kay-Kay, her mom, her dad, and her brother Charlie come walking into the soccer area with baskets of food and goodies. They wave their hands and invite all the fans of both Terminators and Amigos to move in closer.

At the same time, Diesel, Grease and Joe Finerty come into the area, carrying a large trophy case. Joe Finerty makes an announcement. "I'd like to congratulate the Amigos on a great game, and I'd like to offer them my trophy case while they are waiting for Diesel and Grease to build a new one...under my guidance of course. This is how they will repay the Amigo Team for their little soccer-ball stunt before the game."

"What is that trophy case for, Joe?" asks Bibou.

"Well, I did a little stock car racing when I was a lot younger and a lot stupider."

"Oh, I don't think it's stupid to do the things we love," says Bibou. "I think the world would be a better place if people followed the path of their dreams rather than the path lined with dollar bills."

"Hear! Hear!" cheers the crowd.

Diesel and Grease walk up to Emily and Ming who are surrounded by happy fans. Emily sees them and smiles. "Did you guys get to see the game?"

"See the game? Are you kidding? I feel like we were in the game! Didn't you hear us cheering?"

"Sure, we did, Diesel. I was just kidding. Those cheers were great, and they gave us a lot of support to play harder," says Emily.

Grease jumps into the conversation. "Me and Diesel wrote all those cheers."

"I like the one about, 'Amigo team is world best team!" says Ming.

"You like that one?"

"Yeah," says Ming.

"I wrote that one!" says Grease.

"That very creative, Grease." says Ming.

Diesel says, "Hey, we know you guys are busy, and they are going to present you with the trophy pretty soon. But, uh...there's something me and Grease wanted to know."

"Sure, Diesel. Go ahead." says Emily.

"Well, you probably didn't know this, but there's a co-ed soccer team here in Cincinnati, and me and Grease are on that team."

"Oh, that's great. We didn't know that," says Emily and then asks, "What's the name of your team?"

"The Winners," says Diesel.

"But we don't win much," pouts Grease; "Maybe we should change the name to, *The Losers*."

Diesel says, "We didn't win one game all year. The girls that play on our team aren't very good. So...we were thinkin'..."

"Yeah, our brains were thinkin' this together...at the same time, unbelievable," adds Grease proudly.

Diesel takes over, "We were thinkin' that if you and Ming would come over and play on our co-ed team, we might win a few games."

Grease adds, "Heck, we'd probably win *all* our games!"

Diesel says sadly, "Oh, but I guess you're probably too busy with the Amigos and your schoolwork and your horse and dog and all that stuff."

Emily says, "Yeah...we are pretty busy. What do you think, Ming?"

Ming says, "Well, I probably think what you probably think, Emily."

"Wow," says Grease, "I think your minds work together like me and Diesel."

"Oh, wow," jokes Emily, "That much synchrony? I think that..."

Diesel cuts off Emily: "Emily, what where you thinkin' just before Grease cut you off.

Grease, don't blow it, Man!"

Emily motions to Ming: "Ming, come over here. Give us a few seconds fellas." Emily and Ming step away from the boys and talk quietly. They laugh a few times but keep a serious attitude. Then they walk back over to Diesel and Grease. "Well, fellas," says Emily, "We have a few specific concerns, conditions and/or stipulations that would have to be met before we can make our final decision."

"Just to let you know," says Ming, "We lean in 'yes' direction."

Grease looks at Diesel and shrugs his shoulders as if he didn't understand. "I think that means you're thinkin' 'Yes'; is that right?" asks Diesel.

"Yes. Leaning more to the affirmative and less to the negative, I would say," adds Emily.

"Oh, boy! Oh, boy!" Diesel and Grease cheer. "Let us know what your concerns are about...your conditions. We'll do *anything*! Anytime! Anywhere! We know we could beat anybody with you two on our team!"

"Ok, here goes, fellas," says Emily, "Know that we are serious about these stipulations, so listen closely."

"Ok," says Diesel, "Go ahead, we're listening."

Emily says, "Number 1, you must never be mean to anyone again— that means, girls, boys, older people...anybody! Get it?"

Diesel and Grease say together: "Yeah! We got it. We'll be really good and kind to people. We promise."

Just then a soccer ball from the Terminator's team rolls over and stops in front of Grease. He picks it up, and it looks like he is going to kick it over the fence. Diesel yells at him, "Grease! What are you doin'? Think man!"

Grease says, "Oh, yeah...sorry." He picks up the ball and hands it to the Terminator player and says, "Here's your soccer ball. Nice game you played. Better luck next time."

The Terminator girl says, "Thank you. We'll need more than luck to beat soccer players like these two," as she points to Emily and Ming.

Emily says, "Your team played hard. It was a good game. We're looking forward to our next game."

"Yeah, me too. See ya next time," she says walking away.

"Ok, fellas, #2" says, Ming. "You must never ever push anybody again...especially girls."

"Ok, we promise we won't never do that again. We're sorry about that," says Diesel.

Grease goes over and stands by Diesel. "Ok, for payback, you can push me over, Diesel, if you want to...right now if you wanna."

"If you *wanna*?" mimics Emily. "That won't be necessary but that brings us to #3. This is very important. You have to start speaking correct English."

"How we gonna do that?" asks Grease.

"How are we '*going to do that*,' you ask?" says Emily. "It's easy. You listen to your teachers and people who speak proper English and you repeat what they say quietly to yourself until it becomes second nature to you. That's how."

"Is that all your concerns?" asks Diesel.

"That's just beginning," says Ming, "We probably add more as time goes on."

"Is that fair?" asks Grease.

"Absolutely!" exclaims Ming. "If you want us on your team." Ming goes over to Emily and whispers something in her ear.

Emily smiles and says to Grease, "Grease, the next stipulation is, Ming wants to know what your real name is. She says, 'surely, your real name isn't Grease, is it?'"

Grease says shyly, "Not really."

"Well then tell us." Smiles Emily.

"Oh, NO!" shudders Diesel, "We're never gonna...going to live this down."

"Take it easy, Diesel. It's very important," says Emily.

Grease asks, "Why didn't Ming ask me?"

Ming whispers to Emily again. Emily says, "It's a Chinese thing."

Diesel pleads, "Couldn't you maybe substitute something else for Grease's name request? Maybe like uh ah..."

Emily says, "Diesel! If that's the way you want to start a sporting relationship, I don't think we can accept those kinds of terms. What do you say, Ming?"

Ming says strongly, "I say: No Name! No Game!"

Grease says, "Well, in that case I guess we have to give in to that strip...strip-you...what-ever. I'll tell her. But everybody else has to cover their ears."

"Oh, yes, everyone please, please cover your ears!" shouts Diesel as he shakes his head and securely covers his ears.

Emily instructs, "Ok, everyone cover your ears please," as she turns around to everyone and *winks*.

"You don't have to cover your ears, Emily. You might have to explain something to Ming," Grease says politely.

"Ok, Grease...or whoever you are, let us have it," says Ming.

Nervously, Grease prepares to say his real name. Softly and slowly with a quivering voice, Grease speaks. "My name given to me by my Mother, rest her soul...is....my name is... Hum...Hum... Humphrey."

Everyone in listening range, obviously not having their ears covered securely, starts applauding, whistling and shouting! "Great! Humphrey! Humphrey! Humphrey! Great! No more, Grease! No more, Grease!"

Grease cannot believe what he is hearing or seeing. A little choked up with emotion he keeps saying, "Thank you...thank you...thank you very much."

When the crowd settles down, Ming walks up to Grease and says, "Humphrey...that beautiful name. It has music quality. It very strong yet tender like breathing of strong horse. What it mean in English?"

Grease shrugs his shoulders and then looks at Diesel.

"Don't look at me, brother. I didn't give it to you. Now! Tell me. How in the heck are we ever gonna live this down?"

Ming turns around to the crowd. "Anyone know what Humphrey mean in English?"

Everyone shakes their heads. Then Bibou moves out of the crowd. He has his cell phone out. "I know what it means. Googled it. It is a great name, a powerful name. A name that is loved by every American. He reads, "The name is derived from two Germanic words, *Hun* which means 'warrior' and *frid* which means 'peaceful.' So, it means 'Peaceful Warrior.'"

People applaud meaningfully.

Bibou puts away his phone. "It is a name that was born to the American public in the 1940's, a time of trials and tribulations in our country. This name was carried by an actor who played characters who were brave, courageous, fearless, tough and kind...but mostly kind. America loves this name. Congratulations Humphrey...be proud of it...Peaceful Warrior." Bibou shakes his hand.

Everyone applauds. Ming goes over and gives Humphrey a kiss on the cheek. Humphrey wipes his cheek with the back of his hand and then gives everyone a big blushing smile.

Emily speaks, "Actually, we have one more request."

"Another one? No! No," grunts Diesel. "There's gotta be a limit!" Then Diesel shakes his head, calms himself and takes a couple of deep breaths. "Ok, ok...What is it?"

"We'll leave this last one open ended at this time," says Emily. "We'll see how you do with these three to start with. We don't want to burden you with too much responsibility."

Diesel says, "Speaking of responsibility, we've got a little problem ourselves and maybe you can help us out. Could we talk to you both in private, please?"

Emily says, "Since you put it so nicely...sure, we can step over there. Will everyone excuse us for a moment. Thank you."

Emily, Ming, Diesel and Humphrey walk away from the crowd. Emily asks, "What is it, Diesel. It sounds serious.?"

Diesel becomes serious. "It is serious. Well, Grease...."

Ming correcting Diesel says, "Uh...Humphrey, please."

Diesel says, "Ok...Humphrey...is having a little trouble in school. He's not going to move on to the next grade if he doesn't learn his alphabet."

Humphrey gets embarrassed, "Hey man! I know the alphabet! I know all the letters...most of 'em. I mean 'most of *them*; don't know them in the order everybody else does. Big DEAL!"

Diesel says, "You know what my Dad said. If you don't learn the alphabet, you'll never pass and graduate from high school and you'll never get a decent job."

Emily says, "Humphrey, do you like animals?"

Humphrey says, "Yeah, I love animals."

"Well, if you love animals, you won't have to worry about a job. My brother, Charlie is going to be the Zookeeper at the Cincinnati Zoo when he graduates from college. But he's already started looking for people to train to work for him. In fact, right now he's looking for a strong guy to clean out the Gorilla's Cage."

Humphrey's eyes get big. "The Gorilla cage? With the Gorilla still in it?"

"I'm pretty sure," Emily smiles to Ming.

"Oh, my gosh! I better start learnin' that alphabet. I tell you what. I'll show you what I know now and then you and Ming can see how you can help me. What helps me is if I put the letters in a little saying."

"Ok, Humphrey. Good idea. Let's hear it," says Ming.

Humphrey stands up straight, takes a deep breath and starts. "I Saw Giddy Fab Hi Jackin A Very Mellow Extremely Yellow Pony While He Was Sleepin...zzzzzzz. Did I get'em all?"

Diesel, Ming and Emily laugh. Emily says, "I think you got most of them, Humphrey. But I think I didn't hear a Q or U or T."

Humphrey thinks, "Ok, Ok, I got it! If I had a 'Squirt' in there, I think I've got it covered."

Emily smiles, "Very good idea, Humphrey. Your brain is working overtime. But I think we have to tweak your presentation a little more main-stream, so your teacher will be more inclined to pass you."

Humphrey lowers his head. "Ok, ok...whatever you say. Anything to get you on our team."

Kay-Kay calls everybody from the refreshment table. "Hey, kids come on over here for some celebration treats. Emily, why don't you go over and invite the rest of the Terminator team over for some treats? I made plenty for everybody."

Suddenly, an attractive woman walks up to a group of Amigos who are still congratulating one another. She is dressed in very fine, high-end, sporty attire—more than a little overdressed for a soccer match of young girls. Suddenly Veronica, with wide open eyes addresses the newcomer— "Mother!" What a surprise! I didn't know you were coming to the tournament. Daddy didn't tell me."

"Oh, he doesn't know everything, Honey. I saw you kick the ball into the net. That was fantastic. Did you hurt your foot?"

Embarrassed, Veronica says, "No, Mother."

"Well, I must say, your hair looked great, and, unbelievably, it's still holding its shape. I didn't know volleyball was such a rugged sport."

"Soccer, Mother. Soccer."

"Oh, yes. Sorry. Silly me. Now I remember, volleyball is like bowling...right, Veronica?"

Under her breath, Veronica says, "*Whatever*", and then aloud, "Everybody! This is my Mother, Barbara Fitzgerald."

Barbara goes around greeting each girl and tapping them on their heads as she profusely congratulates them all. After commending them all, she pulls a 'Sani-Wipe' from her purse, wipes her hands, then pinching it between two fingers gives it to Veronica. Then Barbara says, "I was so proud of you young ladies and the way you beat that terrible Exterminator team."

"Terminators, Mother. Not exterminators."

"Did I say Exterminators? How silly of me...regardless, we just had our cabin in the Rockies exterminated for some little things that got in and ate all my *hors d'oeuvres* ... oh, don't even want to think about it.... Well, whoever they are, Exterminators or Prosecutors, they deserve to be beaten. Number one, because they weren't a very pleasant group, and two, what hairdos! They look like a bunch of boys out there and number three, PLEASE! those outfits were actually nauseating."

"Mother..."

"Please, Veronica let your mother finish! As I was saying, I was watching you girls running around out there, and something just flashed in my mind. It would look so adorable if each one of you were in a beautiful Veronica Dove creation of mine. It would be so exquisitely stunning, like a dancing rainbow on the green grass and flowers. I've got some catalogs in my car, and I want each one of you to pick out a dress...now you don't have to pick the same one. This is not a team thing. It's just for you. So just be extemporaneous. Take a look, and later write your name, address, phone number and dress size. If you're not sure of your dress size just ask me and I'll tell you. This is what I do, I'm good at it and...I love it!"

"Oh, thank you so much Mrs. Fitzgerald," all the Amigos cheer.

"No, no, no, just call me Barbara. And while we're at it we should think of getting you some new team jerseys. Don't you feel those ones you're wearing are really exhibiting who you really are...agree? Raise your hands if you agree."

All the girls raise their hands.

"Mother, Daddy *just bought* those brand-new jerseys for our team."

"Oh, my goodness...no wonder. He thinks he's Giorgio Armani. Well, this Taco team is going..."

"Amigos! Mother! Amigos!"

"Oh, what did I say...doesn't matter. Watching sports always makes me hungry even though I rarely know what's going on. And girls, put down your jersey size. I'll design a few things, and you can each vote."

Kay-Kay comes up to Barbara, "Barbara won't you please come

over and try some of our treats—everyone seems to be enjoying them."

"Treats? Well thank you. hope they're not off my diet...are they?"

"You know, my doctor recently told me that if you're outside at a sporting celebration...diet doesn't count."

"Oh, good...please, could I have the name of your doctor?"

Ming comes up the refreshment table. "Could I sample some of your beautiful food, Kay-Kay?"

"Of course. Help yourself."

Barbara looks at Ming. "I don't believe I've met you. I saw you out there kicking that ball around. You're very good. My name is Barbara. What's yours?"

"Hi, my name Ming."

Charlie walks up and starts tasting treats. He's close enough to overhear their conversation.

"Oh," says Barbara. "I think I used to know someone whose name was Ming. No, actually I think it was Ming Ming."

"That not me," says Ming. "I only one Ming." She smiles at Barbara.

"Oh...well I wonder who that could have been?"

Charlie interjects, "May I make a suggestion? Perhaps you were thinking of Ming Ming, the giant panda in China. She was the world's oldest panda. Usually wild pandas live about 15 years. Ming Ming lived 34 years. Giant pandas are among the world's most endangered species. There are only about 1,600 in the wild and 300 in captivity in China."

Barbara smiles at Charlie, "My you certainly are a smart young man. Have you ever met my daughter, Veronica?"

"No, I haven't," says Charlie.

"Then I'll have to introduce you later. Oh, by the way, what is your shirt size?"

Ming jumps in to save the day. "Oh, look Barbara. Veronica

lost ribbon in hair. It blowing all over soccer field."

"The ribbon or her hair?" Barbara asks. "Both, I think," says Ming. "Better hurry!"

"Oh, yes...thank you, thank you Ming Ming."

Barbara takes off running. Ming winks at Charlie as they are both start laughing.

"Thanks, Ming. I owe you one," says Charlie.

Kay-Kay rings a little bell and makes an announcement. "Please, everyone gather around. I made a special treat for my grand-daughter, Emily, and I'd like all of you to see it."

Kay-Kay reaches under the table and brings up a beautifully decorated box with pictures of soccer balls all over it and the words, "Champion Amigos!"

"Kay-Kay is that for Me?" asks Emily.

"Who else, Emily? We want everyone to know that Emily's favorite food is pasta...plain pasta of all things. We call her, 'The lover of pasta.' Emily, the Italians are going to make you the patron saint of spaghetti! Go ahead and open it."

Very delicately, Emily unwraps the box and looks inside. "Oh, my. It looks like..." She reaches inside with both hands and pulls out a plate that has what looks like a soccer ball made of spaghetti on it. "How did you make that, Kay-Kay? It's beautiful! Too beautiful to eat!"

Kay-Kay smiles proudly, "Thank you, Emily. I'm sure you'll get over the beauty of it soon and devour it all in no time! Here's the way I made it: First, I baked a small round loaf of bread. Then I cooked several pounds of spaghetti pasta and wrapped the round bread ball with the pasta. After that, I got some vegetable coloring and painted it as a pasta soccer ball."

"You are so creative Kay-Kay."

"Thank you, Emily."

"It's a good thing we won," says Emily.

"There was no question in my mind about the Amigos becoming the champions," smiles Kay-Kay.

All the Amigos and the Terminators gathered around the table and started sampling all the sweets and fruits. Kay-Kay has made a dessert that looks delicious to all the soccer players. It is served in a small paper cup with a plastic spoon inserted. The kids start sampling it and are raving about how delicious it is. Humphrey comes up to the table and looks at the little cups. "What's that?" asks Humphrey.

"Oh, that's what I call my apple berry crumble," answers Kay-Kay.

"Could I try one? I'm not one of the Amigos, but I play soccer with the boys."

Kay-Kay smiles at Humphrey. "Oh yes, but I saw you leading the Amigo fans in cheering on the Amigo team. Am I correct?"

"You got that right!"

"Well, then go right ahead. Enjoy."

Humphrey picks up a small cup. He takes a big spoonful and inserts it into his mouth. His eyes get big, and his smile stretches from ear to ear. "Wow! This is the best thing I've ever tasted in my life! Can I have another one to give to my cousin?"

"Sure, go ahead," says Kay-Kay handing him another one.

Emily and Ming come up behind Humphrey and watch him devouring the dessert. Kay-Kay smiles as she watches Humphrey gulp down another dessert.

"What you eating, Humphrey?" asks Ming.

"I don't know but it sure is good. You better get one before they're all gone."

Humphrey addresses Kay-Kay: "I tell you, Ma'am. This is either the best dessert I ever had in my life or it's so close to it, I can't tell the difference."

"Well, thank you ever so much, Humphrey."

Emily asks her Grandmother, "Kay-Kay what do you call these little cupcake items?"

Kay-Kay smiles, "I call it my apple berry crumble. Please, you and Ming try one."

Emily and Ming enthusiastically pick up an apple berry crumble and dig in. "Wow, Kay-Kay this is heavenly. How did you make it?" asks Emily.

"Well, like the title says—I slightly cooked some apples, berries, blueberries, blackberries, raspberries and put them in a graham cracker crust. Oh, I almost forgot. I've got some vanilla yogurt I can put on the top." They each hold out their apple berry crumble as Kay-Kay spoons some vanilla yogurt on top.

Kay-Kay puts a half spoonful on Humphrey's dessert and the one he carries for Diesel. He cautiously tastes it, "Man-a-live! I didn't think this stuff could get any better. It's fantastic! What did you call it?"

Kay-Kay says, "Apple berry crumble."

Emily and Ming respond. "Apple berry crumble!"

"I have to find Diesel and give him his 'apple berry crumble," says Humphrey and walks away repeating, "Apple berry crumble!

Apple berry crumble! apple berry crumble!"

Suddenly, Emily gets very excited. "Kay-Kay have you seen, Bibou?"

"Yes, Honey, I think I saw him over there by the bleachers talking to Dr. Yang."

"Kay-Kay, you better stay here and take care of the stampede that's about to happen as soon as Humphrey gets the word out about the 'apple berry crumble!'"

"It really great, Kay-Kay," smiles Ming.

Emily, excited with an idea, nudges Ming, "Come on Ming we've got some work to do...fast!"

"Emily? Don't feel like work now. What it is?" asks Ming.

"You'll want to work when I tell you what it is. Oh, there's Bibou! Let's hurry...come on!"

Emily and Ming run toward Bibou as Emily calls out to him, "Bibou! Bibou! Come here! Quickly! You've got to help us!"

Bibou excuses himself from Dr. Yang and runs over to Emily and Ming. "What's the matter, girls?"

Excitedly they quietly whisper to Bibou as they move him to a more private area.

Coach Bob of the Terminators picks up two drinks from the refreshment table and walks over to where Coach Brady is talking to several of his friends. He walks behind Coach Brady and whispers in his ear, "Coach Brady, I wonder if I could have a minute with you."

"Actually, Coach Bob, you can have as many minutes with me as you'd like."

"Thank you, Sir," says Coach Bob as he hands one of the drinks to Coach Brady.

Coach Bob holds up his cup, and then Coach Brady holds up his cup. "I salute you Coach Brady and congratulate you on winning the championship today and especially on building a team of fine young women into a remarkable soccer team. It is truly a reflection of all your talents—your compassion, your insight, and your foresight."

"Coming from you, Coach Bob, that is truly a compliment. I'll keep it treasured in my heart along with all the other wonderful things that have come my way since I started coaching girls' soccer."

"*Salute*," says Coach Bob. "But don't worry...we'll be back next year to win us one just like it."

"And *salute*' to you Coach Bob. We'll be waiting for you." They both laugh, touch cups and drink with laughter.

"You'll have to excuse me, Coach Brady. I've got a little job to do." Coach Bob goes over to the benches, steps up a few levels and makes an announcement. "Everyone please gather around. I have an important announcement." Everyone gathers around Coach Bob. Emily, Ming and Bibou join the group. Coach Bob holds up his hands to quiet everyone down. "The Mayor's office just called me. The Mayor was going to send over a representative to present the trophy to the winner of today's tournament. Well, we know how things get messed up in politics, and they informed me that no one will be able to come and make the trophy presentation to the Amigo team. So, if no one objects, I'd like the honor of presenting this fine trophy to the Amigo team. Veronica..."

The crowd cheers and applauds.

Coach Bob invites the Amigo team to come in close. They all stand on the first step of the bleachers and face the crowd so everyone can see them. Coach Bob holds one side of the trophy and invites Veronica to hold the other. People are taking many pictures and Veronica's mother motions Veronica to fix her hair.

"I want to start off by saying that today I feel honored and privileged to have coached the team that played hard against this wonderful Amigo team. I'm proud of them, and I think they should be proud of themselves. I also want to say that I don't think one trophy is enough. I believe each one of these young ladies on the Amigo team should have a trophy of her own. This Amigo team is a shining example of what soccer *should* be. It's a tough, hard, competitive game with a lot of pushing and shoving, but as I've learned today, it's something beyond that. It's a game of the heart. It gives us a microscopic view of life. When the goodness, sharing and caring of the heart becomes an integral part of the game, then everyone is a winner. Even though my team is said to be the loser, we feel we have won even more than a trophy by coming here to Cincinnati and meeting all you incredible people. As someone said to me just a few minutes ago...sharing this 'dance of soccer' with all you kind, compassionate, and, (I've never heard this word before in a soccer speech, but I'm going to say it now), *loving* people—is an experience I will treasure for the rest of my life. Congratulations to the Amigos and to all their family and friends. Thank you from me, and from my team." He hands the trophy to Veronica.

Veronica holds the trophy high over her head and says, "Thank you very much for those kind and touching words Coach Bob. I am so proud to be called the Captain of the Amigos. We all are the body of this Amigo soccer team. Some of us are the arms, some the feet, the brains, the eyes and everything else, and want to humbly say right now...as the Captain of this wonderful soccer team...the way Emily and Ming played out there today, they have definitely proven to all of us that they are truly the heart and soul of the Amigos."

With that, the crowd applauds and cheers louder than ever for a long time. Tears flow, the wind awakens the trees, and even the leaves seem to be applauding.

Emily and Ming go up to Humphrey and say to him, "Humphrey, we've got good news for you."

"More good news. I don't think I can take any more."

"Well," says, Emily, "Ming, my grandfather Bibou and I have been working on your alphabetic presentation and we've come up with a new saying for you that might help you remember the correct sequence of the alphabet."

"Wow, you did that for me?"

Ming says, "Why not, we're all practically soccer teammates, aren't we?"

"I guess so."

"Come on over here, Bibou. We're going to present this new alphabet jingle to Humphrey."

Emily, Ming and Bibou stand together and look at a piece of paper and say, "Listen carefully, Humphrey. Here goes."

They say it slowly and distinctly, so Humphrey catches every word. "apple berry crumble, Don't Ever Fight, Good Humphrey Is Jolly, Kind, Loving, Miraculously Nice, Overly Polite, Quietly Reserved, Somewhat Timid, Utterly Valiant, and Worships Exotic, Yellow, Zucchini."

Humphrey is very happy. "I'm going to go right home after this and start memorizing. Can I have that piece of paper to take with me?"

Emily hands Humphrey the paper. "Good luck, Humphrey."

"Luck is for leprechauns. I'm gonna...'going' to make this work. Thank you all so much for such a wonderful day. I feel like a different person because of all of you."

Bibou steps forward. "You *are* a different person, Humphrey. And we are all better people for having met you and for being part of this wonderful day with you."

"This is the first time in my life that I feel like a winner," smiles Humphrey.

All the Amigos and fans applaud Humphrey and cheer, "You are a winner Humphrey. You are a winner!"

Emily starts waving her arms and gets everyone's attention. "Listen everybody! Now that we finally know Grease's real name, don't you think it's only fair that we find out what Diesel's real name is?"

Everyone claps, whistles and shouts, "Yes! Yes! Yes! Let's hear it Diesel. Tell us! Tell us!"

Diesel starts stomping around in circles. "Diesel's my real name. That's it! I don't have any other name. Diesel...that's it...that's it!"

Seeing the flustered state Diesel is in, Emily continues her interrogation in a gentler manner. "Well, Diesel won't you please tell us how you got that name? We'd all love to hear the story. Right everybody?"

"Can't we talk about somethin' more interestin' like winnin' the soccer game an' forget about this dumb question?"

Emily won't let Diesel squirm out of this predicament. "We're talking about something interesting, Diesel. We're talking about you! That's very important to all of us. Can't you be a little more cooperative? Soccer teammates are always cooperative with each other. That's what makes a soccer team run like a *well-oiled machine*...to use your lingo...but then, of course, maybe you'd like to rethink the co-ed soccer team. Huh? Would you, Diesel?

Just then, Joe Finerty steps in with a big smile on his face. "Since I'm the father of this young man, I think I should clear up this situation once and for all—because me and my wife had a lot to do with Diesel's name."

"Thank you, Joe. That sounds great!" says Emily. "Now I know we'll get the real story."

"Awe come on Dad! What-a-ya-doin'?"

Not paying any attention to Diesel, Joe swings a tall chair around, grabs the back, and mounts it like a weather-beaten cowboy ready to go out and ride the range one more time. "You see, folks, Diesel's name is a name that grew out of a lotta different situations. My father's name was Dean and my grandfather's name was Cecil. Now here's the story of putting a lot'a different sounds in a blender, turning it on and seeing what you come up with."

"Do you have to tell this story, Dad?"

"I like this story an' I think the world should know it."

"Oh, brother," exclaims Diesel.

"Well," says, Joe, "My mother, Diesel's grandma, lived with us when Diesel was growing up. She, like many older people who didn't have regular dental treatments, lost a number of teeth as time went on. She loved to call Diesel, Dean-Cecil: Dean for my father and Cecil for my grandfather. It made her think of the family she loved, and it was a thing of respect with that generation—not like today when everybody's got a short nick name. Just a 'nick' of their whole name.

"In those days, everybody in America ate breakfast at about 7am, lunch at 12 noon and supper at 6:00 P.M. Life basically stopped at those times. People sat down around a table together, chewed their food, and shared with their family what was happening in their lives. My mother, Ethel Finerty, did a lot of the cooking 'cause both me and my wife had jobs. I had my wrecking yard, and Diesel's mom was a waitress at the local restaurant. My mother took the 'position' of queen of the roost. She made sure everybody was at the table at the appointed times, and she served the fixin's she'd worked hard all day preparin' in the kitchen.

"So, at mealtimes, especially lunch and dinner, she'd get on the back porch and call everybody's name through the screen door! As time went on, and fewer teeth were left in her mouth, Dean-Cecil became Dee Cecil...Dee Cecil became Dcecil...Dcecil became Deceel and finally it all became Diesel. Pretty soon, everybody was calling him Diesel...

"Every so often I'd land a job drivin' a big 18-wheel semi, and I'd take Diesel on a couple'a-day's journey with me. He was just a little fella, and he'd stand on the seat between my legs, grab the steering wheel and think he was driving this big 18-wheeler all by himself. Of course, I had the bottom of the steering wheel in my hands. What he'd like to do is, every time we pulled into one of those big gas stations where all the truckers filled up their rigs, he'd pull the rope on the air horn, and all the truckers would know that Diesel was comin' in for a fill up.

"One time a scary thing happened. We were haulin' a big load of fresh cut logs through Colorado and up the 10,000 feet Laramie Mountains of Wyoming. This was before 'runaway truck ramps' were built in America.

"The fall day was clear and cold, and we were drivin' downhill out of a mountain pass behind another big 18-wheeler haulin' logs like us. Suddenly, we noticed his 'porch lights' were blinkin'. That's what they call the hazard lights on those big rigs, and we knew somethin' was really wrong because at that time there were no exit roads to turn off on up there at 10,000 feet.

"'We gotta get ahead of him,' I told Diesel. 'I gotta move into the hammer lane, that's the left lane, so I can get a signal from the driver.' I moved into the hammer lane, and when I was side by side with the driver of the big 18-wheeler, he looked at me with fear in his eyes and slid his finger across his throat which means, 'I got no breaks!' I tell Diesel, 'I gotta get in front of him, slow down nice and easy, let him touch our back side and then we'll piggyback his big rig all the way down the mountain.'

"I remember Diesel sayin, 'That sounds like fun, Dad!'

"I told 'im. 'This is serious stuff, Diesel. We gotta do this right son, or a lotta people could get hurt real bad or even worse than that.'

"We were up over 9,000 feet at that time. We were *doin' a dollar*, that's 60 miles per hour. By the time I was gonna be in front of our new friend, I'd be doin' at least 75 with a big load'a logs. I don't call that fun.

"I started to maneuver my truck in front of the run-away, and when I finally got around the front of him, I wasn't gonna take my eyes off the road to see how fast I was goin'. I slowed down as gently as I could and then we finally felt him bump our back side. Diesel started clappin' and hollerin'. 'We got 'im Dad! We got 'im on our back!'

"I told him, 'It's not over yet, son. We gotta long windin' road to go. So, what I want you to do is start prayin' the Lord's Prayer out loud, like your grandma taught ya.'

"'Why?' he asked.

"'Cause, you know what they call it when you're piggybackin' another login' truck down a big mountain like this?'

'No,' he said in a shaky voice. 'What'a they call it?'

"'They call it, 'ridin' the devil!'

"Diesel said it over and over, real slow several times...'Ridin' the devil...ridin' the devil.'

"Then Diesel got real serious an' started prayin' the Lord's Prayer out loud...but he just kept repeatin' the same words over and over: *Our Father who art in Heaven...Our Father who art in Heaven.* I think he was so scared he couldn't remember the rest.

"With the Lord's help, we finally got'er down the mountain, and we pulled into the first big fill-up station we came to. In the trucker's world, news travels real fast. When I turned off our rig, like always, Diesel grabbed the horn rope. He was so excited to be off the mountain that he started pullin' on that rope like our truck was on fire!

"It finally became evident that the word had already reached ground level because when Diesel started soundin' our horn all the truckers at the station responded by soundin' their horns. I tell ya it sounded like some kind'a diesel-truck symphony. When we got inside everybody was waitin' for us.

"The men were applaudin', whistlin' and callin' out 'Diesel! Diesel!' and the driver of the truck we helped down the mountain was a big 250 pounder. He lifted Diesel up on his shoulders and went around the store grabin' everything he could carry in his big arms: hot dogs, potato chips, soda pop and Diesel started eatin' everything he could get his hands on as the truckers kept chanting his name: 'Diesel, Diesel, Diesel.' So, I guess right then and there is where he got his name and it's stuck with him ever since. I was really proud of that young fella that night, and after that he always said, he was gonna be a 'big-jimmy driver.'"

Everybody at the soccer match started chanting, "Diesel! Diesel! Diesel!"

Emily gets an idea and motions to Dr. Yang who is close by. "Dr. Yang can you come over here for a minute?"

Dr. Yang walks over to their little group. "What can I do for you, Emily?"

"Remember you told me that one day you were going to tell me the story of how losing can be winning? You haven't forgotten your promise, have you?"

"I certainly have not, Emily."

"Good! Because to me, today seems to be the perfect time for you to tell us all that story."

"You're right. But wait, I have a little different idea. I was wanting to invite you and your family over to our house for an informal gathering. I think this afternoon might be a wonderful time to continue the celebration at our home. It looks like all the rest of the Amigos are with family and friends so we could have our own little private party. What do you think?"

"I think that would be wonderful. Why don't I go tell my mom and dad and see what they say? Oh, do you think it would be ok if Diesel, Humphrey, and Joe Finerty could come along?"

"Splendid idea, because it's a story about things we have all experienced on this soccer field today: courage, joy and most of all—not giving up under any circumstances."

On the way over to talk to her parents, Emily, along with Ming, say 'goodbye' and give hugs to all their teammates and families. Emily sees her mom, dad, and grandparents gathering up all the left-over treats. Emily and Ming run over to them and give them big hugs as they excitedly tell them about Dr. Yang's idea for a get together. Emily's mom gives Emily and Ming a big hug, and Emily turns to Dr. Yang and gives him two thumbs up.

INSIDE DR. YANG'S HOME

At the gathering, the guests wander around Dr. Yang's home, admiring all the Chinese artifacts—the silk wall-hanging that tells the story of the black bird going into the forest with the moonlight on his wings; the pictures of Ming and others playing soccer; the statues of Buddha, until gradually everyone ends up clustered around the statue of *Quan Yin*...mesmerized.

Dr. Yang and Ming quickly make some tea and bring it out to the group in a beautiful Chinese tea service. Dr. Yang and Ming pass the small teacups around. Dr. Yang explains, "In China we have a tea ceremony at significant events. It is called *jing cha*. It means 'to respectfully offer tea.' So, this afternoon we want to respectfully honor our wonderful soccer players, Emily and Ming, and all the wonderful fans and families who attended the game. Also, we kindly thank you for honoring our home with your presence. We hope you enjoy the delicate flavor of the tea we brought from China. It is mostly a blend of Jasmine Dragon Pearls, highest quality in China, and we add a few green tea leaves. By the way, it is very good for your health. It is full of antioxidants, which help the body get rid of waste products in our cells. The jasmine aroma is associated with calmness and peace that helps to settle the body and mind after a very exciting day, which I think we all have had. Please begin to enjoy."

"Dr. Yang," says Kay-Kay, "I brought a few treats that were left over from the soccer match. I was *hoping* we'd have some tea. With your permission, I'd like to offer them in the tea ceremony, if that's appropriate."

"I think we're all familiar with the old saying, *when you're in Cincinnati do as the Ohioan's do.*"

"Thank you, Dr. Yang. I thought you might be okay with them, so I gave them to Ming when we came in."

Humphrey gets a big smile on his face and says, "Oh, boy, some more apple berry crumble."

Everyone chuckles as Ming moves into the kitchen and brings out a large cookie platter full of treats. As everyone is enjoying the tea and the sweets, Dr. Yang stands up and address the gathering. "This story is a true story. It's about a horse."

Emily shouts, "Oh great, it's about a horse! I didn't know that! Thank you. Thank you. *Xie, xie!*"

Dr. Yang continues, "I call this story, 'When losing is winning.' Ming and I were there to experience it." Everyone applauds and Ming has a smile on her face.

Dr. Yang continues. "It was in the summer of 2003 in Japan. Ming was a very little girl then. It was a difficult time for many Japanese citizens. They had suffered hardships for 10 years because of economic problems. The period became known as 'the lost decade.' But there was a beacon of hope in a racehorse named Haru Urara—which means in Japanese, *Glorious Spring*. She was a mare who became a symbol of strength and courage because she had a very long losing streak but never gave up. In 100 races, Haru Urara had never won a race. She became known as 'The Shining Star of Losers Everywhere.'

"She wore a pink 'Hello Kitty' mask and she became symbol of hope all over Japan. She had an incredible spirit. She reminded everyone to try their hardest even if they don't succeed.

"The racetrack where Haru Urara raced was in a rural area in the south of Japan. The track was getting ready to close because people were careful with what little money they had. People were also moving to bigger cities in search of work. Yet Haru Urara, in her pink 'Hello Kitty' mask would still trot energetically out to the track and give her all in every race, despite her fame as a *noble failure*.

"The owner of the racetrack didn't know what to do to save his racetrack, so he put out a story about Haru Urara in all the small newspapers of Japan. The story announced that there was going to be a special race to celebrate Haru's 100th race. The story spread like wildfire throughout Japan. As the day grew closer to Haru's 100th race she was actually running better in every race. People were thinking she could win. Even the Prime Minister put a quote in the news, 'I'd like to see her win!'

"Ticket sales got better every day. A man who was working in his basement at odd jobs because he couldn't find work, scraped up enough money to go to the track and buy a ticket. He didn't bet. He just wanted the ticket for the hope and courage that he would find a job.

"A woman with a very difficult disease came to the track on the day of the race. She had been ready to give up and take her own life. But Haru gave her courage to not give up. She got courage from Haru. Haru was a star of hope for the sad people of Japan.

"People, 1,500 of them, came from all over Japan to see Haru Urara's 100th race. They wanted to see once and for all if Haru Urara could win a horse race. The owner had even hired the best jockey in Japan to ride Haru Urara. The jockey wore a pink satin racing shirt to honor the 'Hello Kitty' mask of Haru Urara. The wives of the jockeys sold, 'Never give up' T-shirts on the day of the race.

"As the starting time approached, it began raining. People became very sad. But just as the race was about to start the sun came out.

"The starting gun fired! They were off. Everyone was excited. Haru was doing well. She was in the middle of the pack. Then unfortunately, little by little, she fell behind. And then, as usual... Haru was last.

"For a short time, the crowd was silent, but soon the whole spirit changed. As Haru passed the stands on her way back to the stable area, the sighs of loss turned into joys of laughter. The crowd became exhilarated. 'Our hats off to Haru!' they shouted. She walked in front of the stands. We all cheered over and over: 'Thank you Haru, thank you!' She had become the shining star for losers everywhere.

"The people cheered, 'Thank you, thank you!' Haru even did a victory lap. The jockey walked her slowly. Haru was proud. The sun was shining on her. The people kept cheering. 'Thank you! Thank you!' They didn't care who won or who lost. They were in love with Haru. She had filled their hearts with hope. Why? Because she gave the people courage—'Never give up!' Even if you don't make it. Never give up. Because then, inside of you, you are a winner! If you can believe that, you become your own fan. Your own cheering section. You are your own trophy.

"The racetrack was able to stay open with all the money the betting people had lost. The track was saved from bankruptcy.

"The owner left with Haru and was never heard from for a long time. Then Haru showed up in 2014 at a small farm outside Tokyo. The farmer asked the public for funds to help support Haru. People remembered and responded. They never forgot the one that *never gave up*—the star of hope for losers. Now she is living in a nice place. She is at peace, eating good grass and eating good food."

As Dr. Yang's story was drawing to a close, a few people wiped their eyes with the napkins they were served.

"Haru never gave up." Dr. Yang continued. "She tried every time. If you feel in your life that you gave your all...not once, but over and over you gave your everything, you should still be commended. You are commended. You are a winner!"

Everyone gently applauds Dr. Yang.

"So, this is the story—*When losing is winning*. Maybe you think I made this up. Google, *Haru Urara* and you'll see for yourself. There is even a video."

As people cheer Dr. Yang again, Emily and Ming motion to Diesel and Humphrey to follow them out of the room into the hallway. The guests start to say goodbye to Dr. Yang and congratulate him on the telling of the *Haru Urara* story.

Bursting back into the room, dancing with enthusiasm, Diesel and Humphrey shout together, "We got 'em! We got 'em! We got Emily and Ming on our co-ed soccer team. We are going to be champs like the Amigos! Unbelievable!"

Everyone joins in, laughing and congratulating the boys, and sharing the excitement of the kids.

As the guests begin to leave Dr. Yang's home, they thank him again for his kindness and hospitality. Slowly walking out, they breathe in deeply the fresh evening air. As they look up, they see they are surrounded by giant trees that stand as sentries for the small innocent dwelling that is painted beautifully by the pink light of the full April moon. The thrills of the day are soothed by the gentle comfort of the warm summer night.

Emily goes over to Ming and says, "Wow what a day, huh?"

Ming says, "Yeah, huh!"

Emily responds, "My mind is spinning with joy! I don't think I'll be able to sleep tonight."

Ming answers, "Who want to sleep?"

Emily comes back with, "My thoughts exactly. Do you want to do something fun?"

Ming says, "The funner the better! Like what?"

Emily suggests, "Well, we've got a couple of nice horses, a real sweet dog, and a beautiful full moon out there. I tell you what. Why don't we race out to the lake, and if you beat me, I'll tell you the meaning of 'she-nancy-she-cans'. You ask your dad, and I'll ask my mom, and we'll meet back here in a few minutes."

Ming says, "Deal!"

Emily goes up to her mom. "Mom, Ming and I'd like to ride out to the lake for a little bit and kind of let the excitement of this day settle down. What do you think?"

Emily's mom looks sweetly into Emily's eyes, "Emily, today is a day when you could ask me for anything, and I wouldn't be able to say 'no.' You and Ming just go, have fun, and be careful."

Ming returns and comes up to Emily. "My dad say, *Mei Wanti*."

Emily smiles, "Great! Let's go get the horses!"

Returning to Emily's house, they enter the stable, mount their horses, and start toward the lake. As they near the lake, Emily and Ming start racing neck and neck with great gusto. Fritz keeps up the best he can. As they get closer to the water, Emily gently pulls back on the reins of Pegasus and lets Ming go ahead of her. Then Emily calls to Ming. "Pull up, Ming."

Smiling, Ming pulls her horse to a stop. "Well, Ming it looks like you're the winner. But before I tell you about the 'she-nancy-she-cans', I was just thinking about this bright full moon. What if we wait quietly at the lake's edge till it's really dark? Maybe a wide-winged blackbird will fly out of the forest, gather the full-moon light on his wings, and then we can watch him fly over our heads. He'll fly back into the woods to light the night with the moonlight on his wings, so the beautiful birds can see to gather their food. What do you think, Ming?"

"I not see why not. I think totally possible. Because today is day of miracles! Giddy up!"

"Giddy-up!" shouts Emily as they race to the lake in the full-moon forest.

GLOSSARY

BANANA KICK – Kicking the side of the soccer ball to make it curve like a banana.

BICYCLE KICK: Performing a backflip, the soccer player flips herself high into the air and kicks the soccer ball while she is upside down in the air, i.e., from over her head and above her waist.

BUTTERFLY: The soccer player kicks the ball when "suspended" in midair with all limbs stretched out like a butterfly.

DRIBBLING: The way a soccer player keeps the soccer ball under her control as she maneuvers down the field, running through and around her opponents with very tricky foot work.

FLIP THROW: A powerful technique of throwing the soccer ball back into play. The player stands 10 feet behind the out-of-bounds line. With both hands, she holds the soccer ball above her head, then runs with great speed and plants the ball on the ground a few feet behind the out-of-bounds line. Then—she flips her body over the ball and lands on both feet without touching the out-of-bounds line—catapulting the soccer ball back into play with one violent whipping motion.

NUTMEG: Kicking the soccer ball between the legs of the defensive opponent with great dexterity.

PIROUETTE: Ballet term for spinning around on one leg—the other leg is off the ground and can be either straight or bent.

RAINBOW KICK: To get out of a tight situation, the soccer player scoots the ball up her leg to knee level, then with her opposite heel, kicks it up into the air so that the soccer ball arcs neatly over her head—while her opponent is trying to figure out where the soccer ball went.

SAMBA: A quick change of pace, rhythm and direction to outsmart defenders.

ACKNOWLEDGEMENTS

Emily Hall,

John and Kay Berno,

Drawings by Michael Berno—

Editing by Angela Mailander, Kathy Butler,

And thanks to Dr. Hongjian He, Dr. Shang Liang—my Chinese Acupuncture Teachers

And for inspiration, Clara Berno *

www.ingramcontent.com/pod-product-compliance
Lightning Source LLC
Chambersburg PA
CBHW051139260626
47170CB00005B/1881